'You an[d] [...]
commitment t[...]

KNOWSLEY LIBRARIES

KNOWSLEY
METROPOLITAN BOROUGH

Please return this book on or before the date shown below

You may return this book to any Knowsley Library

everything.'

Laura Martin lives in a small Gloucestershire village with her husband, two young children and a lively sheepdog! Laura has a great love of interior design and, together with her husband, has recently completed the renovation of their Victorian cottage. Her hobbies include gardening, the theatre, music and reading, and she finds great pleasure and inspiration from walking daily in the beautiful countryside around her home.

Recent titles by the same author:

HIS PERFECT PARTNER

COMING HOME
FOR CHRISTMAS

BY
LAURA MARTIN

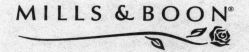

MILLS & BOON®

First published in Great Britain 1998
Harlequin Mills & Boon Limited,
Eton House, 18-24 Paradise Road, Richmond, Surrey TW9 1SR

© Laura Martin 1998

ISBN 0 263 81308 8

26463721

Set in Times Roman 10 on 10½ pt.
02-9812-57674 C1

Printed and bound in Norway
by AIT Trondheim AS, Trondheim

CHAPTER ONE

IT WAS going to be a beautiful day: crisp and cold, with sunshine glinting magically on frost-laden branches.

Refreshing. Invigorating. Josie had a sudden compulsion to dance and run and scamper about like a five-year-old.

She didn't, of course. Grown-ups weren't allowed to do things like that, were they? Besides, scampering about wasn't the same when you were alone. You needed someone to chase, or to be chased—an equally crazy mate, or giggling children who could share in the fun.

Josie removed her brimmed hat and shook out her silky blonde hair. She felt warm. The climb along the woodland path had been steep and difficult in places—not many people chose to push on this far, which was a shame, because if they only knew how magnificent the view was from here...

Josie's mouth curved into a happy smile as she gazed out across the valley below. It looked wonderful, just as it always did. Every hill, every tree, every blade of grass—she loved it all. She couldn't imagine a day when she would ever take any of this for granted.

She breathed out a long, contented sigh, allowing her gaze to focus on one particular spot, savouring the moment as usual.

There it was, settled in the fold of the valley, nestling quietly between the village of Harcombe and the larger town of Eastford.

A wonderful, wonderful house, alone, undisturbed, surrounded by trees on one side and gently undulating fields on another. The perfect family home—or at least it would be one day; it was old and dilapidated now, of course, uninviting, uncared for. But Josie had dreams...such dreams...

Harcombe Hall. Waiting to be saved.

Josie released a tense breath, threw her head back and stared up at the glacial blue sky overhead. It had been so hard concentrating on work all week—poor Susan definitely thought she was losing her mind. But as the date for the auction crept ever nearer she had found it virtually impossible to concentrate properly.

'Not long now,' she whispered. 'Soon. Very soon...' She glanced at her wristwatch and quickly calculated. Only six hours to go, then all the planning and hard work would come to fruition.

She crossed her fingers and closed her eyes tightly, praying that everything would work out. She wouldn't allow herself to dwell on the unthinkable, the fact that she might not purchase Harcombe Hall. She couldn't bear it. No, she must stay positive. She wasn't a fool. She was a business woman, and a good one at that. This wasn't just some silly pipe dream. She had done her homework. She knew what the likely selling price at auction would be and she was prepared to match it, almost double it if necessary, to get what she wanted. Success this afternoon would be her reward for working all the hours God had given her for the past seven years, for giving up any decent kind of social life.

For being alone.

Josie tossed her soft green hat in the air, caught it expertly and, with one last backward glance at Harcombe Hall, skipped along the track which looped around the wood and would take her back towards the tiny car park in the valley below.

She sang as she went. The late autumn sun was such a tonic. Who cared that it was absolutely freezing cold? Better like this than the dreary rain and dull, leaden skies which they had had to endure recently. Fitting to have such glorious blue skies and sunshine on this day of all days. If she forgot the cold nipping at her toes, and ignored the puff of cold smoke every time she released a breath, she could almost pretend it was summer...

Now there was a thought—and a much used one at that. Summer at Harcombe Hall—one of her favourite images: a picnic on manicured lawns, a baby sleeping peaceably in a pram nearby, tiny children playing in the sunshine, their father, the man she loved with every ounce of her soul, holding her in his arms...

Josie sighed wistfully. That was where the image became a bit hazy—deliberately so. The fear that it might never happen... She wouldn't put a face or a figure to the man of her dreams. It was too difficult. Too impossible. The fantasy of having someone to love, a man who cared about her with equal heart-stopping intensity...

Besides, hadn't she spent enough years wasting precious hours and minutes on something that could never be?

Don't spoil it! Josie admonished herself silently. One thing at a time. The purchase of the house would be a start. And there was plenty of time—she was only twenty-five. Years and years left in which to find the man of her dreams, to have those sweet, angelic children, with their masses of bubbly blonde hair...

I'm mad! she thought, blue eyes shining. Absolutely mad... Successful business woman who can only dream about true love and motherhood? Thank goodness nobody else knows what's going on inside my head!

Her sweet voice soared as she strode along the path. Josie concentrated on everything except where she was going: the crystallised canopy of trees overhead, a frosted spider's web, a squirrel darting along a branch...

Matthew really didn't expect to meet anyone out here this early in the morning. Particularly not a blonde-haired beauty with a penchant for Gilbert and Sullivan. He paused and watched her lithe body swinging along, a smile automatically curving his lips. She looked happy, whoever she was: full of joy and vigour and vitality.

He released a heavy sigh and his smile disappeared momentarily, so that the handsome face looked serious, almost daunting, with its strong, classical features and dark, brooding eyes.

He felt suddenly old and tired—very tired; that was the trouble. Not helped, of course, by the delay on his flight—too many hours spent in a depressing airport lounge and a quick-fix hotel. Not to mention the endless nights spent tossing and turning as he'd tried to come up with a solution to a problem that seemed if not insurmountable, then pretty close to it. His first priority had to be the children. Kathryn was having a hard time, and he felt sorry for her, would do the best that he could for her, but ultimately Josh and Abbie were the only ones that mattered in all of this.

He followed the girl's progress, aware that just looking at her skipping along the woodland path lifted his spirits immeasurably.

Had he ever possessed anything even approaching such enthusiasm, such verve? Maybe, but it felt like a lifetime ago.

He debated whether to move on, knowing the girl would feel awkward at having had an unknown admirer in this most relaxed of moments, especially one who was feeling so disgustingly morose. The path she was travelling would eventually bring her to this very spot. He had a couple more seconds, then he really had to move if he didn't want to cause her embarrassment.

Hell! He wished he could turn the clock back. He had known pressure before; his life revolved around it—making deals, getting projects in on time. But that was business, and this was different. This was about people and stability and happiness, and most of all the future of two sweet children.

Matthew released a breath. Hell! What was wrong with him? He had to lighten up. Things weren't so bad. He was just tired, that was all. Just tired...

'Nice tune.'

Josie skidded to a halt at the sound of an unexpected voice. Oh, goodness! What was she doing? Bad enough skip-

ping about like a child and warbling like an over-excited
nightingale without someone having seen her!

She blushed scarlet, looked around her, saw the flash of
a stunning smile, friendly, attractive...

Familiar?

'*The Pirates of Penzance*—am I right?'

'Y-yes...'

Her first thought was, Handsome, her second thought was,
Handsome, and her third...

She swallowed and inhaled a sudden breath. *It was him.*
The flush that was suffusing her face grew deeper. Her third
thought was, Matthew. Here. In front of her. After all this
time.

She hardly dared believe it. It couldn't be, could it? *Ten
years.* She risked a closer scrutiny; he looked different, older,
wiser—the usual sort of thing. But the essentials hadn't
changed. Still those wonderful dark eyes which crinkled
when he smiled, the same deeply sensuous mouth...

Josie swallowed hard and wondered vaguely if the excitement of the day was making her hallucinate. She met the
dark gaze and felt the flip of her heart—an automatic reaction and one that she had never been able to conquer, not in
all the years, not even now.

She needed to speak again, to say something else. He was
beginning to look at her as if she were a little mad...

'You must think me...crazy, singing to myself out here
all alone!' Josie gulped another breath and tried to appear
vaguely calm.

'You didn't sound crazy—just happy.' He smiled, and her
heart flipped again; it was still there, that stunningly attractive twist to his mouth which Josie remembered and loved
so well. 'Seems a pretty good reason for singing,' he added
lightly.

'I...I didn't think...anyone else would be here.' She could
hardly get the words out. Her heart was banging away inside
her chest. Could he see it? Did he understand what he was

doing to her, *had* done to her by appearing out of the blue like this?

'I didn't mean to embarrass you.'

'You didn't! Well…' Josie corrected herself. 'I suppose you did a bit…' Her voice trailed to a halt. She couldn't drag her eyes away from his face now, so mesmerised was she by the vision of him standing before her. There was a pause. The silence of the wood echoed in her ears, deafening her.

'Matthew?' His name, not uttered for so many years, was a breathless, unbelieving query on her lips. 'It is you, isn't it?'

His brow creased faintly, the velvety dark eyes narrowing a little as he looked at her. It was only then—in that moment of hesitation—that Josie considered the awful possibility that he might not remember her. After all, why should he? Ten years was a long time, and she had been just another friend of Sheila's—a good friend, but to an older, unattainable brother little more than one of many giggling schoolgirls.

She stepped back a little, needing more space. His presence still had the same effect on her: as if oxygen was in short supply, as if her knees were no longer quite good enough at holding her upright. 'Sorry! Now I've embarrassed *you*,' she murmured. 'You won't remember me—of course you won't—!'

'Josie?'

He did. Her mouth curved into a smile. The relief as he spoke her name was immense. It was almost all she could do to stop herself bursting into song again. *Thank you*, she whispered silently. Thank you so much…

'Well…this is…' His smile had vanished; dark, suddenly sombre eyes moved over her face in slow assessment. 'A surprise, to say the least.'

Uncertainty replaced the surge of happiness. He wasn't pleased to see her. Too many memories of those times—the times he had chosen to leave behind. She should have pretended—ignored the fact that Matthew was here, standing only feet away after so long.

'You haven't changed.'

'Really?' Josie tried hard to hide her disappointment. 'Not even a small bit?' she queried. 'The last time you saw me I was a fifteen-year-old schoolgirl with braces and pigtails!' She struggled to play it bright and cheerful, managing somehow, but only just. 'You know, for a moment I felt awful because I didn't think you were going to recognise me. Now I recall what I looked like in those days and I almost wish you hadn't!'

Matthew's mouth twisted in the attractive, lazy way she remembered so well. 'All the women I know would give anything to stay as young-looking as you.'

'Would they?'

All the women... For a moment reality reared its ugly head. Ten years of all the women Matt had known and loved raced into Josie's mind. Yes, she admitted realistically, there would have been plenty: glamorous, sophisticated, intelligent... A great wave of depression swept over her suddenly.

'Oh, well... In that case...I'll try and take it as a compliment, then!' she replied stiltedly.

Stunning eyes held hers. 'Which is how it was meant.'

There was a pause. It lengthened. Josie frantically tried to think of something to say. She didn't want any awkward silences; she didn't want this conversation to end before it had begun.

'So...how are you?' she asked finally, despairing at her own lack of imagination.

'Me? Oh...not bad.' He had hesitated, it wasn't lost on Josie—nothing about Matthew Jordan was lost on her. Beneath the lethally assured outer shell he looked tired, she noticed. Fraught, tense. 'What about yourself?' he asked smoothly. 'You're looking...' his eyes traversed her body in swift appraisal '...well.'

Drat and double drat! Josie cursed inwardly. She didn't want to look 'well.' She wanted to look stunning, ravishing, memorable. *Fat chance of that!* Of all the rotten timing. Josie glanced down at herself. She had on her oldest, most un-appealing clothes: scuffed boots, faded jeans and a decidedly worn padded jacket. And there wasn't a scrap of make-up on her face.

'If this is 'well' then I'm a Chinaman!' Josie retorted. She knew how she had to play it now, if she wanted to keep her dignity and pride intact: cheery, brisk, matter-of-fact. Just two acquaintances meeting briefly after a long time apart. 'I woke up this morning, saw it was going to be a nice day,' she added, just a little too quickly, 'threw myself out of bed, jumped in the shower and came straight here on my bike. I must look an absolute wreck!'

He couldn't remember having seen anyone so fresh and lovely in a long while—the quintessential English rose; that was what she was. Utterly beguiling. Josie. Sheila's friend. He remembered her, of course, but only just. His memories of those times had never been particularly good, and over the last few years he had tried to block them out completely. But now...

Matthew stared down at his outstretched hand, cursing inwardly. What on earth was he trying to shake hands with her for? He made amends, pulling her close, once her slender fingers were safely ensconced in his, to plant a kiss of greeting on her cold, reddened cheek.

Her skin was soft. He could smell the fragrance of her freshly washed hair. It felt good to be close to her. Special.

Like coming home.

Josie's insides flipped a triple somersault. He had taken her breath away. She couldn't believe she was this close to him after so long. He smelled gorgeous: the subtle aroma of co-logne mixed with freshly washed skin, the masculine scent of him... His kiss was gentle, platonic, but the vibrancy which he exuded, the magnetism of his whole wonderful self, left Josie totally mesmerised.

'So!' He stood back, surveying her with undisguised interest, with a twist of a smile, that told Josie he had finally remembered how to tease. 'Do you come here often?'

'Yes.' Josie finally remembered to breathe. 'Every week!'

She knew she was blushing, couldn't believe the extent to which shyness had overwhelmed her. She turned swiftly, glancing around the wood, desperate for a moment in which to compose herself. 'It's wonderful here, don't you think?' she announced conversationally. 'It lifts the spirits. There was a squirrel back there.' Josie kept her gaze fixed on the way she had come. 'He had a nut in his paws and he was nibbling so daintily. Do you call them paws?' She glanced back, saw the undertone of amusement in Matthew's expression, looked away again, carried on hastily. 'No matter. But he looked so sweet, and he just sat on a branch, nibbling away, watching me. And I saw a woodpecker too—a black and red one—' She halted abruptly. The wood was noticeably quiet now that she had stopped prattling on. Oh, drat! Here she was, desperate to impress, and instead she was reverting back to the gauche, awkward schoolgirl Matthew had known and probably hated.

Nerves. That was what it was. Ten years on and he was still capable of turning her into a gibbering moron.

'Sorry!' she announced self-consciously.

Matthew looked suitably surprised. 'What for?'

Josie threw him a knowing look. 'For talking like an idiot, that's what!'

'It all sounded like perfect sense to me.'

'And there's me imagining the curve to your lips has something to do with the fact that you find me amusing!' Josie retorted swiftly. 'That inside you're laughing at me.'

'Never that.' Matthew's gaze was suddenly serious. 'But you make me smile. You haven't changed, Josie James,' he added gently. 'Still young and fresh and full of vigour.'

'You make me sound like a puppy, or...or some sort of...of vegetable!' she retorted desperately.

'Not a vegetable.' Dark eyes sparkled as he looked at her. Amusement returned, lifting his features, so that it wasn't difficult to remember the young Matthew again. 'A flower, maybe. A daisy, perhaps, or a daffodil. Yes.' He considered her with mock seriousness. 'Definitely a daffodil; they're bright and sunny—'

'And unsophisticated,' Josie finished flatly.

There was a noticeable pause. 'Who wants sophistication?' His voice changed suddenly, hardened, if only a little. 'Always an overrated quality, in my opinion.'

'Oh, yes?' She allowed her gaze to wander over his casual but undeniably expensive clothes: a dark, supple leather jacket worn over a rich green cashmere jumper and faded jeans. Quality boots, the glimpse of an expensive watch at his wrist. It wasn't difficult to assess the sort of lifestyle he had: good—better than good—great, most probably.

'Meaning?' Matthew's expression was suddenly rather formidable.

'You look as if the years have been kind to you,' Josie replied. 'I mean...your clothes...' She was struggling, and Matthew knew it. 'They look very expensive.' She gulped a breath, and allowed her gaze to feast upon his magnificent figure. 'Sophisticated,' she added lamely.

'You think so?' Dark brows were raised in query. 'The words 'book' and 'cover' spring suddenly to mind,' Matthew drawled.

She sensed the change in him, was aware of a hint of steel in his voice. Heat scorched Josie's face. 'Sorry. I didn't mean to imply—or to assume anything—'

'No, don't be.' Matthew released a tense breath. 'It's me that should be apologising.' He shook his dark head slightly. 'Sorry, I didn't meant to bite your head off. I'm feeling a little wound up at the moment...' He smiled briefly. 'The victim of not much sleep and quite a bit of jet lag.'

'Really?' Where had he been for the past ten years? Josie

wondered. Abroad, clearly. Not that it mattered. Unattainable, that was what he was…always had been and probably
always would be. He might as well have been on the moon.
'Where have you come from?'

'South America.'

'Nice!' Josie didn't bother to hide her interest. 'Which
part?'

'Mexico. Before that Peru, then Brazil, Chile, Argentina.'
He lifted his shoulders in a slight shrug. 'You name it…'

Josie arched a brow. 'Not one long string of holidays, I
presume?'

'No…work. I'm a structural engineer,' he offered with a
smile. 'In case you're wondering.'

Josie grinned. 'I was.'

'You know, all the years I lived in this area,' Matthew
added suddenly, 'I don't think I ever stepped inside this
wood—foolish, wasn't it?' He bent and picked up an acorn
from the ground, turned to her smiling. His voice was light,
but Josie sensed… What, exactly? she asked herself. Difficult
to pinpoint, but there was something about the features beneath the smile, the line of his shoulders, the tautness in his
frame…

'Yes, I'd say it was.'

Her gaze rested on his hands: strong and tanned and in-
herently masculine. He was turning the acorn over and over
between his thumb and forefinger, like a worry stone.

Back in England now. Maybe this was the first time he
had returned. The memories would be strong and painful. It
would be difficult not to think of Sheila with every step he
took. 'But then I'm biased,' she continued evenly. 'I've always loved this place. I tend to think of it as my own personal piece of countryside. I get quite put out when I come
across other people.

Sensuous dark eyes held hers. 'Me?'

Her stomach flipped. Josie shook her head. 'No. No, of
course not you!' she replied quickly. 'It's a wonderful place,'

she added swiftly, aware of Matthew's compelling gaze. 'There are great views.'

'Yes, I noticed. I was looking earlier,' he murmured. 'I'm glad there hasn't been too much development over the years. The valley and surrounding area looks pretty much as I remember. Sheila always liked coming here, didn't she?'

It was a relief that he had mentioned her. To have met and not mentioned her name would have felt like a crime. Josie smiled, glad to be able to talk about the one person that linked them. 'Yes. We used to walk Bruno here most evenings after school—run over all the usual gossip together. Of course, that was in the early days...' Josie hesitated a fraction, and then forced herself to continue. 'Before her illness was diagnosed.'

'Yes.'

Silence. Josie watched as Matthew inhaled a deep breath. 'I still miss her,' she murmured quietly.

Melting dark eyes held hers. 'So do I.'

There was a long pause. Then Matthew added briskly, 'Did you know our dear aunt had Bruno put down once Sheila died? I only found that out recently.' He threw the acorn he was holding far into the wood. Josie listened for the rustle of leaves as it landed in the undergrowth. 'Typical, of course, but still depressing. He was a young dog, with plenty more years left in him.'

'Yes.' Josie struggled with the lump in her throat. 'I would have had him. It didn't occur to me that she would... I felt so guilty because I didn't ask.'

'I hope you didn't waste time and energy blaming yourself.' A grim curve twisted his mouth. 'Knowing my kindly aunt, I doubt she would have given him to you anyway.'

'If Sheila hadn't died so suddenly, maybe—'

'Don't!' His voice was terse. He met Josie's startled gaze and shook his head slowly, and his voice was softer when he spoke again. 'Don't,' he repeated. 'It's over now. Finished. There's nothing we can do.'

'I know.' Josie nodded, forcing a watery smile. She hadn't

expected to feel like this now—not after so long. Maybe it was because of Matthew, appearing out of nowhere, his presence transporting her back to those teenage days which should have been full of fun, and had been on occasions, but also filled with sadness.

'So!' She made a gigantic effort and smiled cheerfully.

'So?' He looked at her. And there was the teasing light back in his gaze again. 'Shall we walk?'

They fell into step, strolling together side by side. It seemed totally miraculous to Josie that he should be here, that she should be walking beside him like this. After so long, she thought. So long...

Silence fell between them. Josie wondered if Matthew was still thinking about his sister, and all the bad times which had caused him to leave so suddenly after Sheila's death.

'What does the day ahead hold for you, Josie James— work or play?'

The suddenness of his question made her hesitate for a moment. Josie's heart skipped a beat as she thought of the auction that afternoon. In the excitement of seeing Matthew again she had almost forgotten it. 'Oh...a mixture of things. I'll probably go into work later...and there's something I have to do later in the afternoon.'

'Connected with work?'

'Er...yes, sort of.'

He found himself wanting to know about her. Everything— from the silliest of details to the not so silly...

Where did he begin? There were no rings on her fingers— she wasn't married. Not that that signified a great deal these days—she could be involved in the passionate affair to end all passionate affairs...

Stop it! he warned himself silently. Don't even think about it. Hadn't he vowed to keep things simple over the next few months—*not* to get involved with anyone, however tempted he might be...?

He had to keep this light, keep things easy...

*   *   *

'So, Josie James? What have you been doing with yourself all these years? No, let me guess.' His teasing voice sounded strained to his own ears. 'You used to be a bit of an academic star, didn't you? I remember wishing for some of your brains when it came time to revise for my exams.'

'You didn't!'

'Oh, yes!' Matthew smiled at Josie's obvious astonishment. 'You were a straight A student, as far as I can remember. Sheila broadcast your exam results loud and clear—she was as pleased as you must have been. So, what is it?' he added, more seriously. 'Brain surgeon? Rocket scientist? Doctor? Lawyer?'

'None of those.' Josie trailed her finger along a branch and watched as the frost collected like snow on her glove.

'No? What, then?'

'I…I work in an employment agency,' she told him quietly. 'Well, not work, in exactly—'

'An employment agency?' Matthew repeated. There was an edge of astonishment to his voice. It wasn't difficult to surmise in the silence which followed that her reply had clearly come as something of a shock.

'And you…you like your work?'

'Yes. Very much so.' Josie couldn't disguise the edge to her voice. 'Is there something wrong with that?' she added bluntly.

'No, of course not. Not at all.'

'But an employment agency?' Josie arched a brow in query. 'Not quite what you expected?'

'*I* didn't expect anything.' Matthew's gaze was steady and unflinching. 'If I remember correctly, Sheila told me it was *you* who had the expectations.'

'You think I've failed.' Josie stared at the frosted crisscross of branches dead ahead and kept her voice deliberately calm, deliberately neutral.

'I didn't say that!'

'No, but you thought it,' Josie replied, a little bitterly.

'I *thought* you had plans to go to university?'

'I did.'

Dark eyes surveyed her face. 'So what happened?'

'I didn't get there.' She was being obtuse. Now why was that? Why was she being so juvenile all of a sudden?

'You failed your exams.' It was a statement, not a question.

'Yes.' Her reply was brittle. She lifted her shoulders in an unconvincing shrug. 'It happens.'

'Why?'

'Why does it happen?' Josie queried. 'Well, usually because a person isn't clever enough—'

'Oh, come on!' Matt stopped walking and Josie did likewise. His expression revealed sudden, sharp irritation. 'To others, maybe, but not to you! Sheila's death?' he pursued. 'Was that the reason?'

'I really don't see the point in going over this...' Josie thought back to how it had been ten years ago. Losing Sheila, Matthew leaving so suddenly after the funeral...

The pain she had endured—that had been something. Guilt, too. Guilt, because amongst the genuine sorrow for her best friend's death, there had been misery for herself because she had lost Matthew—a man who had hardly been aware of her existence. 'It was a terrible time.' Her voice was barely more than a whisper. She couldn't be anything else but honest. 'I...lost interest. Staying in, studying all the time...' Josie shrugged '...there didn't seem to be much point to it all.'

'Of course there was a point! You were alive! You were young and beautiful and intelligent!'

'Well, I didn't feel particularly alive, and I sure as hell didn't feel particularly intelligent!' Josie flashed angrily. And as for being beautiful, she thought miserably. If I was, then why didn't you notice me? *Why?* 'So I failed my exams and I didn't make it to university. Big deal!' Her eyes met his, accusing him, hating him suddenly, because that was a great deal easier than the alternative. 'Believe it or not, I'm rather pleased with the way my life's turned out!'

'If that's the case, why so defensive?' Matthew asked with cutting clarity. 'Am I right in remembering you were keen to pursue a career in medicine at one time?'

'Childhood fantasies,' Josie replied flatly.

'Only because you weren't prepared to work to make the fantasy a reality,' he commented coolly.

'Look! What is this?' Josie demanded, struggling hard to keep her cool. 'I've got a great life. I'm happy, settled, ful-filled...' Her voice trailed away for a moment. 'Besides—' she attempted a smile, hating the way the conversation had soured '—what do you care?'

He didn't attempt to answer that question—intent, it seemed, on pursuing the fact that in his eyes at least Josie had failed, by settling in an employment agency.

She could tell him now. Throw the success of the agency into his face—*her* agency. Flaunt her achievements and watch the reaction in his eyes: ownership of the fastest-growing employment agency in the south of England; voted 'Young Business Woman of the Year' by a national maga-zine two years in succession.

But something held her back. What was it? Josie struggled to think coherently. Stubbornness? Pride? Annoyance be-cause he had returned and then assumed and accused without giving her the benefit of the doubt? Yes, she admitted, all of those things. Just who the hell did Matthew Jordan think he was—appearing like this out of nowhere, upsetting her equilibrium by criticising the choices she had made? Well, she had moved on, grown up, managed to make something of her life even if he didn't think so. But she'd be damned if she'd tell him now. She had no need to look for his ap-proval; she wasn't some kind of puppy, longing for a pat on the head.

'I just can't believe you gave up.'

'I couldn't believe it when you ran away!'

Josie inhaled a sharp breath. The words were out, and she couldn't haul them back inside.

There was a lengthy pause. 'You think I should have

stayed?' Matthew's voice was controlled, his eyes were cool and watchful.

'I shouldn't have said that,' Josie murmured. 'It's none of my business. Anyway,' she added quickly, hating this new direction the conversation had taken as much as the previous one, 'it was a long time ago.'

'You haven't answered my question.' Matthew's gaze was steady, his voice infuriatingly calm.

'Maybe I don't want to!' Josie replied with spirit, then, 'OK! Yes!' she added heatedly. 'Yes. For whatever it's worth, I think you should have stayed!'

'I see.'

No, he didn't. Not at all, Josie thought miserably.

'I didn't have the strength, or the energy—not back then,' Matthew stated flatly. 'Besides,' he added with unwitting brutality, 'what was there to keep me here?'

Me. Josie lowered her head, lacking the courage to look into his handsome face again.

Just me, she repeated silently.

CHAPTER TWO

A CERTAIN amount of interest had been generated in the sale, and the auction room was starting to fill up.

Josie took a seat, settling herself on a hard wooden chair at the back of the hall in order to get a good view of the forthcoming proceedings. She felt nervous.

'Nothing to worry about,' she whispered to herself. 'Just stay cool, calm and collected and everything will work out fine.'

She had to believe it. Oh, there was bound to be an element of risk, buying a house at auction, but that, she told herself forcibly, was all part of the fun. Anyway, she was here on time, she had the financial side of the operation worked out, and the auctioneer was just mounting the platform. As long as an earthquake didn't hit, or she didn't drop down dead with heart failure—an occurrence that felt quite possible at that moment, given the state of her heart-rate—she didn't see why everything shouldn't go to plan.

She felt more confident now too, more like her old self—or rather her new one. The Josie James that Matthew Jordan wasn't aware of.

The meeting with him had left her feeling curiously out of sorts. They had parted awkwardly, abruptly, unable to converse on a lighter level, unwilling, after their disagreement about Josie's choice of career, to pursue anything deeper.

More than simple acquaintances, but not quite friends either.

He had said he would be in touch, but what did that mean? Josie knew what she wanted it to mean, but the chances of that... She exhaled a breath. She couldn't stop

thinking about him, that was the trouble. All the way back
to Eastford, peddling her battered bicycle like a mad-
woman, she had dwelt on their meeting, analysing every
word, every look. Irritated that it should matter so much.

Still.

As soon as she had arrived home she had effected the
transformation from gauche, awkward schoolgirl to sharply
presented business woman, to convince herself that time
hadn't played a trick, that she wasn't plunged back ten
years in history, that she didn't have to live through all that
emotional turmoil again. That she really was a successful,
independent woman of means.

Josie glanced down at the smart navy trouser suit she
wore, checked that her hair—now coiled into a smooth chignon—was still immaculate. Would Matthew Jordan recognise her in this guise if he saw her again? She smiled
faintly. Probably. But he would get one hell of a shock.

The auctioneer was climbing to his rostrum. Josie inhaled
a steadying breath. So many months of planning, so many
years of working all the hours God sent, taking risks to
build up her employment agency so that she could fulfil
her dream of one day owning Harcombe Hall.

It was all that mattered. As a child, living in tatty rented
accomodation, the faded grandeur of the place had been a
glorious lure. Her daydreams about one day living there
had been sharp and clear from the very beginning. It had
been her focus, her escape from a family life which had
often been fraught with tension and uncertainties. How often had her father threatened to leave her mother before
finally walking out? How often had she had to endure the
awfulness of days, weeks on end spent being the go-
between? Josie closed her eyes briefly and let out a sigh
that was pure tension. Too many. But that was all in the
past now, and here she was, on the brink of a wonderful
new phase in her life. The purchase of a family home, a
place that would one day be warm and welcoming and sta-
ble, enduring in a world full of change and upheaval. Never

mind Matthew Jordan's assertions about universtiy and a glittering career in medicine—although both might have been nice. No, the family was what mattered. Some time in the not too distant future she would put right the mistakes her own parents had made; she would have a family and there would be love and security and laughter at Harcombe Hall.

The bidding started slowly. Josie held back in the first instance; time enough to let the main players in this most nerve-racking of dramas show their hands. The price edged upwards; a couple of buyers fell away. Josie felt more confident. She leaned back in her chair and managed to relax a little. She had an upper limit, but there was still plenty of room for manoeuvre left at this stage.

A wave of her brochure and she had made her first bid. Then another, and another. She was beginning to get into her stride, almost to enjoy it.

The price rose steadily. The house had already passed its estimated selling price, but that wasn't an issue. She was prepared for that.

'Thank you, sir.' Another bid from a middle-aged man dressed in a suit, near to the front of the hall. The auctioneer's eyes flitted back to Josie at the back of the room.

No hesitation. Another wave of her brochure and now the bid was with her. She held her breath, waiting as her opponent debated whether to continue or not. A couple of seconds passed and Josie forgot to breathe. The price was high, clearly near to her opponent's limit, given the amount of time he was taking.

Oh, please! she whispered silently. Give up! There'll be other houses. You can't possibly want Harcombe Hall as much as I do.

The man nodded. The auctioneer's gaze switched to Josie. She lifted her brochure without hesitation. The bid was with her once again.

Now a longer hesitation. Josie fixed her eyes on the man. After a lengthy moment he shook his head.

That was it! Outwardly, Josie didn't move a muscle, but inside she was whooping with joy. She tried not to smile, she tried not to show how much it mattered, but the hope and excitement that she had been keeping under strict control for the last few months began bubbling inexorably to the surface.

'With you, madam, at two hundred and thirty thousand pounds!' The auctioneer's voice was authoritative. He raised his gavel expectantly, but it didn't drop as Josie predicted it would. She watched worriedly as his attention was attracted by one of his assistants. 'I have a telephone bid,' he announced to the room. 'Two hundred and fifty thousand pounds!'

Josie's heart thudded. Oh, goodness! What should she do? There was a lot of work still needing to be done on the house, and two hundred and fifty thousand pounds was the limit she had set herself.

She raised her brochure.

'Thank you, madam!' The auctioneer looked pleased, as well he might, considering the amount of commission his firm would receive, Josie thought tensely. 'At two hundred and seventy thousand pounds!' The auctioneer glanced once more to his assistant on the telephone, nodded and continued. 'With the telephone at two-ninety!'

This was awful, like one of the anxious dreams she had had recently where no matter how hard she had tried she simply couldn't attract the auctioneer's attention. Except that was not the problem now, for he was waiting, looking at her, and she was the one dithering, unsure...absolutely petrified...

Should she? Could she possibly afford it? But if she didn't, Harcombe Hall would be gone. *It would not be hers.*

She raised her brochure once again and ignored the feeling of panic in her stomach.

'Three hundred thousand pounds!'

Too much! Too much! a small voice inside her head repeated over and over again. Even if you manage to buy Harcombe Hall, how are you ever going to afford to *live?*

It was too late now anyway; she had done it. Surely this would be it, Josie thought desperately. Who else would pay so much for a run-down country house set in the middle of nowhere?

'With the telephone, at three hundred and thirty thousand pounds!'

Somebody else. That was clear. Josie's heart felt like lead. Well, that was it! She knew when she was beaten. *Three hundred and thirty thousand pounds!*

It was beyond her now. She couldn't possibly go any higher. She shook her head at the auctioneer, lowered her head and gazed forlornly at the brochure with its photograph of Harcombe Hall on her lap.

The sound of the gavel was harsh and unforgiving as the auctioneer declared the property sold.

Gone. She could scarcely believe it. All her plans for the future dissolved in just a few heart-stopping seconds.

She had lost.

Josie rose from her chair. She felt numb, hardly able to comprehend all that had happened. Somehow she found her way out of the stuffy hall and into the crisp October air.

It was chilly. Josie walked on unsteady legs over to her car, which was small, boring, decidedly tatty—transport being another casualty of her determination to save as much money as possible. And for what? she thought miserably.

She fumbled for her keys in her bag and opened the door. No point at all now. She sat quietly behind the steering wheel, reliving the final moments of defeat, then opened her bag and stared down at the crisp banker's warrant inside. Useless now. She picked it up and ripped the cheque into tiny pieces, watching as the worn interior of her much used vehicle became littered with confetti-sized pieces of paper.

She felt lost. Alone. Defeated.

What should she do now? Not go home. Besides, the small box which had never been anything except a temporary place to live wouldn't offer any comfort. No, she couldn't go back there yet. Every harsh angle and badly constructed piece of brickwork would be a reminder of what she had lost.

To the office, then? No, not there either. What was the point? What comfort would she find there? Just a reminder of all the hours she had spent chasing a dream. Too modern anyway, with its chrome fittings and unforgiving red carpet which showed every speck of dirt and had to be vacuumed at least three times a day.

She'd drive; that was what she'd do. Just drive.

Josie started the engine, crunched the car into gear, and roared away from the auction room like a demon possessed.

After an hour, she ended up—foolishly, she knew—at the house. It was like a magnet, drawing her to itself in the chill of the late autumn afternoon.

Josie brought her car to a precarious halt at the side of the road, got out, slammed the door shut, then clambered over the locked gate at the end of the drive, uncaring of the damage she might be doing to her extremely expensive outfit, or of the fact that she was now officially trespassing.

Her heeled shoes crunched desolately on the weed-infested gravel. She strolled up to the tall iron gates which marked the once grand entrance to Harcombe Hall and stared miserably at the heavy padlock.

It was getting dark. Just one last look and then she would force herself to forget all about it. Just one last look…

The old house loomed impressively in the early evening light. The silver moon, half hidden by a bank of low cloud, was partially visible through the skeleton of trees which surrounded the house at the rear.

Josie gripped the iron railings and peered across at the once elegant Georgian building. She still couldn't believe it. *Gone*. What would happen to the old place? Some sort of dreadful scheme, most probably—a health spa, or a nursing home which charged exorbitant fees to those lucky few that could afford it.

She sniffed miserably as the first tears of bitter disappointment trickled silently down her face. At least no one—apart from her bank manager, and Craig, her accountant—had known of her plans for Harcombe Hall. That was some comfort. There would be no pitying looks, no blithe words of commiseration. Nothing.

Josie wiped away her tears with the back of her hand. She tried to think positively, but it was difficult. Maybe somehow, in some way, she would come to see that this was for the best. Maybe she was better lowering her sights a little. Maybe she had had a lucky escape. Maybe it would have been a disaster buying Harcombe Hall.

Maybe she was just kidding herself…

Josie plucked at an overhanging branch and a sprig of early mistletoe came away in her hand. Only a couple of months until Christmas.

She couldn't bear to think about it, but she did anyway. Another dream. Christmas at Harcombe Hall would be special. Blazing log fires, spruce and pine decorating every room, a gigantic fir tree sparkling in the main hall. Oh, she could picture it all so clearly—*had* pictured it a thousand times. And more besides, much more. Children—laughing, squealing in delight as they unwrapped their presents. Josie hugging them close, looking across somewhere to a shadowy figure, smiling tenderly at the man she loved, their father…

She swallowed, struggling against the tightness in her throat. *Stupid, stupid girl!* Get a grip! she admonished herself fiercely. Stop being so pathetic! It wasn't going to happen. Not any of it! She had been living in fantasy-land these past few months. It was about time she realised that—and fast.

It was a moment before she became aware of the footsteps crunching along the track, and by then they were almost upon her. Josie turned quickly, trying to make out a figure in the half-light. A man. Yes, definitely a man! Oh, God! Josie's vivid imagination sprang into horrible life. What on earth was she doing here? She should have done the sensible thing and gone home. Her car was parked on the side of the road like a beacon for any pervert or murderer who might happen to be passing...

He was approaching, she could see the crispness of a white shirt gleaming in the moonlight, the outline of a broad frame.

'H-hello?' Rigid with tension, she decided to brazen it out. 'Who's there?' Her voice was faint and wobbly—hardly likely, she thought worriedly, to deter a potential rapist.

'Don't be concerned. I saw the car at the side of the road. It was parked pretty haphazardly. Is everything OK?'

For a moment Josie couldn't speak; her relief was too great. She closed her eyes and offered up a prayer of thanks. It was Matthew.

'I...I'm just out for a stroll,' she replied croakily, turning away so that she could scrub frantically at her wet face with the sleeve of her jacket. 'Everything's fine.'

'Actually, it's not.'

Josie inhaled a steadying breath. No hint of recognition. Matthew, it seemed, didn't have a clue who he was talking to. Josie hoped she could keep it that way. The mood she was in—well, it would either be a case of snapping his head off or falling into his arms...

'You must know you've got a couple of punctures on the nearside of the car. Isn't that the reason you stopped?'

Josie's heart sank. She kept her face averted and spoke with her sleeve in front of her mouth. 'No, no, I...I didn't. Are you sure?'

'Positive. Front and back, on the passenger side. There must have been glass on the road when you pulled over.'

'Damn!' Josie sniffed, substituting her sleeve for a tissue, dabbing at her damp face, wondering if she could possibly continue to avoid detection.

'Josie?'

Her heart leapt.

Matthew took a step towards her. 'Josie, is that you?'

For a moment she seriously considered trying to deny her own identity. She had very much wanted to see Matthew again—she had wanted him to see *her*. But as the self-assured business woman that she was. Not like this, all emotional and depressed and angry and bitterly disappointed.

'Yes,' she whispered.

He came closer. And in that moment the moon revealed itself from behind the cloud. The silver light shone down upon his broad frame—and the obvious expression of astonishment on his face. 'What on earth are you doing out here all alone like this?'

'Just taking some fresh air.'

'Didn't you get enough this morning?'

She could hear the gentle humour in his voice, but it didn't make her feel any better. At that moment, Josie seriously doubted whether she'd ever laugh again. 'Look, there's nothing to worry about,' she informed him briskly. 'Everything's fine—apart from the punctures anyway. Thank you,' she added. 'I...I just fancied a walk.'

'Another one?'

There was amusement in his voice; somehow it made everything seem twice as bad. 'Yes. Another one.' Josie struggled to keep back more tears. 'Matthew...please—'

'Josie, what is it? Is something the matter?'

'I...' Josie inhaled a breath. 'No, of course not,' she lied. 'I just want to be left alone, that's all.'

'No way.' Matthew's voice was firm. 'I can't leave you out here by yourself—you *are* by yourself?' he persisted, glancing around.

'Yes, of course I am!' she snapped. What was he imagining? Josie wondered. That this was a lovers' stroll, that she had some man hidden in the bushes? The thought made Josie want to cry more, but by some gargantuan effort she managed to stem her tears. It was murder talking to him like this, trying to sound as if she wasn't upset when in reality all she wanted to do was wail aloud like a tormented banshee. 'Matthew, go! Just leave me alone, can't you?'

'Hey!' He came closer, reaching out a hand to touch her damp cheek. She heard a low, succinct curse. 'You're crying!'

'No, I'm not!' She moved her head away, trying to avoid his touch, but his hand was warm and firm against her face. Burning into her. Making her weaken her resolve.

'Josie!' She could hardly breathe. He was so close, so strong. She could feel the warmth of his body, smell the wonderful masculine scent of him. 'What is it?' His voice was gentle, a whisper of kindness in the dark, cold night. He reached down, removed the tissue she was holding and smoothed it gently over her damp cheeks. 'Tell me,' he murmured. 'Maybe I can help.'

'I…I don't want to tell anyone. It's pointless now anyway,' Josie added miserably. 'It's too late.'

'For what?'

'I…I worked so hard…lived like a monk—'

'A monk? Don't you mean a nun?'

'Yes…' She sniffed, and told herself she had to stop crying. 'A nun…' She tried to laugh, but it came out as more of a sob. 'And it was all for nothing. Well, not for nothing exactly, but…it won't be the same now.'

'Sweetheart, I don't know what you're talking about, but surely it's not the end of the world?'

Sweetheart? Matthew had called her sweetheart! Somehow it only served to make her more miserable. *'Don't!'* she whispered. 'Please don't.' Her face crumpled in anguish, and the tears began to flow more copiously.

'Don't what?'

'Be kind. 'It…it just makes me feel worse.'

'Has someone hurt you?' His voice had a steel edge suddenly, as if a thought had just occurred to him and he didn't much like it.

'Yes.'

'Who?' His tone was sharp. 'What have they done?' he gritted.

'I don't know who...' Josie sniffed and shook her head miserably. 'Someone...'

'Josie...you're not making sense.' Matthew tipped her chin and forced her to look at him in the moonlight. 'Have you been attacked?'

'Attacked?' Josie frowned at the thought. 'Oh, no, nothing like that!'

'Had an argument with someone—is there some man?' Matthew continued.

'No.' Josie heaved a breath. 'No,' she repeated dully. *A man?* Oh, God! He hadn't been listening to a word she'd said. If only he knew! She stared up into the taut, dark features.

The irony of it. The only man she'd ever thought about or wanted was him.

Josie remembered how happy she'd been that morning. What a difference a few hours could make. She leant against the tall iron gates, shredding the tissue she held between her manicured fingers. 'Sorry,' she added woodenly, 'for being such a cry-baby. You can go. I'll be OK. I just need time to sort myself out—'

'I told you. I'm not leaving you stranded out here alone.' Matthew's voice was firm. 'Come back with me. I'll give you a lift to wherever it is you want to go.'

'I told you—I'm fine. I don't want to go anywhere!' Now she was being stubborn, and foolish and juvenile again. A reaction, she decided, against Matthew's calm affability.

'Josie...!' His voice held a warning note. A frisson of desire scorched through her body as he came even closer; now there was barely any space between them. Josie looked up into his face, almost marvelling at the fact that she should be this close to him. He threw her a vexed look. 'What's got into you all of a sudden? You're not yourself.'

'How do you know?' Her retort was sharp and unfairly harsh. Josie was aware, in a corner of her mind, of a badly required need to let off steam. Damn him for turning up now! Not just at this moment, but at this time in her life—just when she had begun to really kid herself that everything was slotting into place. This was awful. Ten years he had been gone, and during that time she had had to make a life without him—a good life, but empty at the heart, where it really mattered. Oh, she played the focused business woman, who put her career first and everything else second, because it suited her to do so, because there really was no other option, but deep inside...

Some nights she woke up *aching* to be held—oh, there had been friendships, a couple of disastrous relationships, but none that had ever amounted to anything really serious.

And he didn't have a clue. Had *never* had a clue.

'You're upset.' Matthew's voice was deep, sensuous, gentle. 'I can't leave you on your own.'

'Why not? You left me alone ten years ago!'

'What?'

Josie put her hands to her head and closed her eyes. She hadn't meant to say that. Foolish, foolish girl! She had made it sound as if he had abandoned her, as if there had been some tie between them, as if he had let her down.

Which he had, of course, but unintentionally. How had he been supposed to know—a young man of twenty—that she had felt the way she had? A silly schoolgirl crush; that was what it had been. No, not a crush. Josie sniffed hard, remembering. It had been more than that. Much more. She had spent years trying to deny it. *Years*. She had loved him. Very much. So much it had hurt.

'Please, will you go?' Josie commanded forcibly. 'Stop being so damned caring!'

'What's the matter?' Matthew's voice was tough suddenly, full of restrained anger. 'Don't you like caring?'

'Not from you, no!' Josie turned towards him, glaring in the darkness. Now she was really being silly. Shouting at him. Being unreasonable and ungrateful. It was too late, though. She couldn't take it back. Better to plough onwards, to really dig her furrow deep. 'I don't want or need anything from you!' she continued almost wildly. 'I've got along by myself all these years...' She gulped back a sob, and scrubbed fiercely at her tears. 'You can't bully me! This is a free country. I can stay here if I want to!'

She remembered he could be unpredictable, a little wild—that had been one of his attractions. And the years, it seemed, hadn't changed him as much as she had supposed.

When he dragged her towards the strength of his body, and then lifted Josie clean off her feet, she was so surprised she didn't do or say a thing, except gasp in shock. They were halfway down the drive before she actually found the resource to ask Matthew exactly what it was he thought he was doing.

'Taking you home.'

'I don't want to go home!'

'Taking you to my hotel, then.'

Josie gulped, and decided she should have opted for home. 'Not there either!'

'Too bad!'

She had made him angry. His whole body fizzed with it. Josie could feel the power of him, strong and lean against her own slender form. One hand hooked firmly around her waist, the other supporting her thighs.

Matthew Jordan, she realised belatedly, was in no mood to be argued with.

'I'm...sorry! I shouldn't have been so...so...'

'What?' He glared down at her. His profile was taut in the moonlight. 'Annoying? Childish? Look, something's upset you. You don't want to tell me what it is—I can accept that. What I will not accept is being on the receiving end of your bad temper!'

'Sorry.' She waited, peering into the darkness as he strode along the track towards the road. In a moment he would come to his senses and see that she was quite capable of walking by herself.

'I told you I was tired this morning—well, I sure as hell am still tired now!'

'Well, put me down, then. I didn't ask for you to carry me all this way!' Josie retorted.

'No!'

'But...but I've apologised!'

'So? Maybe I'm choosing not to accept it.'

'You can't do this to me! You can't treat me like I'm some sort of silly girl!' Josie's voice was rising again, each syllable a note higher than the last.

'Stop screeching in my ear—you're deafening me!' There was a sudden hint of humour in his voice now. Josie glanced up into his handsome face.

'You're enjoying this, aren't you?' she accused.

Matthew's mouth curved attractively. 'Now whatever gave you that idea?'

They had reached the gate. Matthew lowered Josie to her feet. 'Capable of climbing over?'

'Of course.'

'Mind your clothes; there's barbed wire along the top in places.'

Josie glared, but it was lost on him in the fading light. 'I got over, didn't I?' she commented huffily.

It was better this way—being angry. Better than crying and feeling utterly miserable. At least it gave her something to focus on.

Defeat. It had definitely left a sour taste in her mouth, and she didn't like it one little bit.

'What are you doing?' She watched, astride the gate, as Matthew walked to her car, reached in, pulled out her keys from the ignition, her handbag from the glove compartment and then proceeded to lock the doors.

'What does it look like? Retrieving your personal belongings and locking the car.'

'I could have done that.'

'True.' He glanced over. 'Do you want help getting over that gate?'

'No.' Josie swung her leg over the top bar and dropped, after some difficulty, to the ground. 'See? Not quite the idiot you so clearly take me for.'

'Your bag and keys.' Matthew held out the offending articles. 'We can phone for a garage to pick up your car from my hotel.'

'Your...hotel?'

'Yes.' He paused for a moment, time enough for Josie to imagine all sorts of scenarios. 'For dinner and a stiff drink. I'm presuming you haven't eaten.' Matthew glanced at his watch in the darkness and she saw the luminous glow. 'It's gone seven. Are you hungry?'

She was—ravenous. Excitement, nerves, and a mixture of Matthew and the auction had meant she hadn't been able to face food all day. 'Yes,' she admitted. 'Yes, very.'

'Good.' He took hold of her hand and tugged her to a long, low car parked behind her own. 'I hate eating alone.'

Alone. Was that what he was? She had been secretly dreading the moment when he would mention someone. A name. His woman. The reason for his return.

'So do I,' Josie murmured quietly, conscious of his fingers, strong and firm, engulfing her slender hand as he pulled her towards his car. 'So do I.'

CHAPTER THREE

'IF I SUGGESTED you lay off the wine, then you'd probably snap my head off, wouldn't you?' Matthew enquired evenly.

Josie picked up her glass with deliberate care and took another mouthful. 'Probably,' she replied lightly. She raised her glass a little and squinted at his stunning handsome face opposite. 'This is incredibly tasty stuff.'

'Too tasty. Maybe I should have chosen something sour and horrible,' he replied dryly. 'Do you often drink this quantity?'

'Me? Oh, yes!' Josie lied, leaning back in her seat, holding her wine glass with exaggerated care as the waiter served them with coffee and liqueurs. 'Often! All the time, in fact!' She smiled. 'I'm a secret alcoholic. Didn't you know?'

'How could I?' Matthew regarded her steadily. 'It's the first time we've met in years—remember?'

How could I forget? Josie thought. She placed her glass very carefully onto the table. Matthew was absolutely right, of course; she had drunk too much. Not on purpose—that wasn't her sort of thing at all. It had just...happened. Too nervous, too tense. A need to do something with her hands and mouth. And now she was suffering for it; her head felt all woozy and her mouth didn't seem to be able to form words properly.

If she wasn't careful she was going to make a complete and utter fool of herself.

'Why did you come back?' At least there were some advantages to her present state, she thought, as she watched Matthew's face for a reaction to her question. Alcohol had a definite knack of making you less inhibited—she wouldn't have dared ask such a question sober. 'As you pointed out earlier, there's nothing here for you, is there?'

He was silent for a long moment, deciding, presumably, how best to answer her question, or indeed whether to answer it at all. 'Did I say that?' he murmured. Josie watched as he picked up the small jug from the table and swirled cream into his coffee.

'Yes, you did,' she informed him. 'This morning, in the wood. Well, then?' Josie could hardly believe her own presumption. All evening she had sat, eating in silence, avoiding questions about herself, determinedly keeping the conversation on general chit-chat, and now here she was, pestering him like this.

Smouldering eyes met her bleary gaze. 'Well, what?'

He didn't look particularly pleased. Not angry, exactly— nothing as extreme as that—just...brooding... Josie hovered a little over her question. 'Why have you...returned?'

'It's as good a place as any to...' His voice trailed away.

'To—what?' she asked lightly.

He looked at her then, a steady, unflinching gaze. 'To settle down.'

Josie stilled. Her fingers gripped hold of her coffee cup and she raised it shakily to her lips. *Settle down?* The dark liquid scalded the back of her throat, and she gasped and spluttered a little.

'Pretty unbelievable, isn't it?' Dark eyes held Josie's face for a moment. He wasn't smiling, she noticed miserably. It definitely wasn't a joke.

'I had a sudden unexplainable desire to return to my roots,' Matthew continued. 'You were right,' he added, spearing her with a look. 'I did run away.'

'On your own?' Josie inhaled quickly. 'I mean...' She frowned, feeling foolish.

She saw the intake of breath, the preoccupied frown, knew in that moment that Matthew was about to shatter all her dreams once and for all. 'No,' he murmured. 'Not on my own.'

'Oh...' She managed finally to get the word past a throat that was suddenly tight and uncomfortable. This had certainly turned into one hell of a day—all her fantasies finally biting the dust. She could feel the glitter of tears pricking her eyelids, and stared very wide, smiled *very* wide. 'Well! Well!' she murmured shakily. 'I had no idea!'

'Why should you?' Matthew's gaze was enigmatic. 'I don't suppose you've ever considered me the type to want to set up home and play happy families.''

Families. Specific. Purposeful. Josie suddenly felt extremely queasy—the quantity of wine consumed, or the shock of Matthew's revelation. She wasn't sure which. Beneath the once crisp lines of her trouser suit, her body was rigid with misery. She tried desperately to think of something to say, but there was nothing she *could* say— only, Who is she? Where did you meet? How much do you love her? Why can't you love me instead?

Pretty juvenile stuff.

'Excuse me...' Josie rose abruptly, swaying slightly, like a tall reed of corn in a faint breeze. She gripped hold of the table momentarily for support. 'I...I think I need to visit the bathroom,' she murmured. She glanced at Matthew, and then pressed her napkin to her mouth as a wave of nausea overcame her and exited the dining room at a run.

He had simply had no idea—no idea that he would meet her again, that she would have this effect on him. He was handling this all wrong. But what was the right way? Fate was playing curious tricks. All these years. So long, so far away...

He had said he would try. He would do it for the children's sake, if nothing else. Security. Love. He understood how important those things were. He couldn't let them down. He couldn't...

*　　*　　*

Josie wasn't sure just how long she spent in the ladies' room. Too long, clearly, because after an indiscriminate length of time she heard Matthew's voice on the other side of the door, asking if she was all right.

Josie gazed at her reflection in the mirror. No, she wasn't—not at all. She looked like a ghost. She hadn't been sick, but it had been touch and go for a while. She felt drained, unaccustomedly inebriated, and totally, totally miserable.

'I'll...be out...in a moment.' She pulled at a tissue from a box near the mirror and wiped the tears and smudged mascara away from around her eyes with a clumsy hand. She had to go out. She had to face him. She had to get through this nightmare somehow.

Oh, but it was going to be so difficult. Why had she come here with him? She screwed her eyes shut tight for a moment. *Why?* She should have seen the danger. Too much wine—the only time in her entire life that she had got herself into this pathetically inebriated state.

Big mistake.

'Here I am!' She tried to play it bright and cheerful, tried to pretend that it didn't matter that Matthew had found love—some woman who meant more to him than she ever would.

But it didn't go to plan. Josie emerged from the ladies' room, caught her heel on an invisible thread in the carpet, tripped, and fell headlong into Matthew's outstretched arms.

In some far-off corner of her mind she was aware of him saying something, of his strong arms around her body, lifting her, of being carried up stairs, along corridors, but she didn't seem able to do anything about it. Not that she *wanted* particularly to do anything. It was wonderful, feeling safe and warm and comforted at last...

She heard a key in a lock, was vaguely aware of a door opening, remembered the bombshell of Matthew loving someone else, whimpered softly like a puppy at the thought, and then sank against the strength of him into much needed oblivion.

Matthew disentangled Josie's arms from around his neck and laid her gently onto the bed. She really didn't look much older than the fifteen-year-old he had left behind. Her hair was messed up, she had mascara under her eyes...

He brushed a gentle finger across her cheek. A totally perplexing mix, that was for sure: fiery one minute, vulnerable the next...

He straightened up, ran a hand over his own face. What was happening to him? Was this some sort of knee-jerk reaction? A distraction to take his mind off what lay ahead? Hell! He felt old—so very old. And tired. Maybe that had a part to play in all this. Maybe he felt this way because she had caught him at a weak moment. And how exactly *did* he feel?

Matthew shook his head. He wouldn't think about it. He mustn't. Not now. His eyes traversed Josie's slim body. Definitely not now.

His gaze fell to her crumpled trousers; there was a tear in the leg—from the gate, presumably. A good suit, by the look of the cloth. Matthew smiled gently. Probably her only one. He knelt down beside the bed and began to slip off the navy blue jacket...

Josie awoke only minutes later—or at least that was what it felt like. But it wasn't minutes that she had been asleep for. Not at all. The bright sunshine streaming through the unknown window told her that. It was much, *much* longer.

The first thing she became aware of was the dull ache of her head, then the horrible dry taste in her mouth.

Then the bed.

Her eyes wouldn't focus properly at first. The sheets were too bright, and the sun was blinding her. Where was she? Not at home, that was for sure.

Then, with a jolt, the experiences of the previous evening came rushing at her and she remembered. All of it—or at least she thought she did.

Josie groaned as she sat up. The sheet fell to her waist. She was wearing just her blouse, and half of the buttons were undone, revealing her bra. She quickly lifted the bedclothes and saw with horror and embarrassment that her trousers had disappeared, and that all she had on were her white lacy briefs.

Josie clutched at her head and looked around Matthew's hotel room with a frantic gaze. It *was* his. She could see the jacket he had been wearing last night folded over a chair. She could hear the distant splash of a shower...

Oh, hell! He would probably emerge at any minute!

With a head that felt as if it were about to fall off, Josie scrambled out of bed. She glanced back at the rumpled sheets, a look of anxious panic on her face. Had he...had they...*just* shared the bed last night? Was that *all* that had happened?

She tried very hard to think, but her brain felt like cold, lumpy porridge. She couldn't find her clothes. What had Matthew done with them when he'd undressed her last night? Or had she undressed herself? The questions spun round and round inside her head. Why hadn't she gone home? Why hadn't he taken her home? Had she been really, *really* stupid? Had there been more to the evening than just dinner and too much to drink?

The door to the adjoining bathroom opened and Josie froze. She looked at Matthew, then wished she hadn't; it just made her feel more aware of...of *everything*.

He looked stunning. There simply was no other description for it. So alive and full of vitality; dressed in denims, with a checked shirt hanging open at the front to reveal a broad, tanned chest, a towel draped around his neck, dark hair wet and gleaming...

'Good morning. How are you feeling?'

For a long moment her mouth seized up completely; she

could feel her jaw hanging open. Eventually she found her voice. 'Like death warmed up.'

'I can't say I'm surprised. That's hangovers for you.' Josie, acutely conscious of her own scantily clad figure, wished her blouse were a little longer. Matthew observed her futile efforts to cover her body with an amused smile. 'I thought you'd want to lie in a little longer, that's why I didn't wake you.'

'Oh!' Josie's gaze was drawn back towards the rumpled bed. She averted her gaze and glanced around the room hastily. 'I can't find my clothes.'

Matthew began drying his hair with the towel. 'I sent them to be cleaned and repaired. You had a tear in the trousers.'

'There really was no need,' she informed him stiffly. His hair was ruffled. She had never seen it that way before. It made him look kind of...vulnerable. She had never seen the flat, muscled planes of his stomach, or the broad, tanned expanse of his chest either, but 'vulnerable' definitely didn't enter the equation as far as those parts of his body were concerned. Josie quickly averted her gaze, conscious of her lingering eyes.

'It seemed a good idea at the time.' His mouth curved. 'Don't worry, I'm sure your suit will be here shortly. Why don't you take a shower? It will help your hangover,' he suggested casually.

'Who says I've got a hangover?' Josie retorted waspishly. 'Anyway, I can't.'

He frowned faintly. 'Why not?'

'I haven't got a change of clothes, that's why!' she hissed desperately. 'What am I supposed to put on afterwards?'

'I'm sure the hotel would send out for some underwear if we asked.' He crossed to the phone by the bed. 'I'll chase up your suit and order breakfast in the meanwhile. There's a robe on the back of the door. Put that on when you've finished showering.'

He seemed to have all the bases covered. Josie watched

as Matthew picked up the receiver, casual, unmoved by the fact that she was standing in the middle of his bedroom half undressed. Naive, that's what I am, Josie thought miserably. Of course he's not fazed. He's thirty, for goodness' sakes! He's been away for a decade. Think how many women he's probably been in this situation with before...

Josie's shoulders drooped. She might as well do as he suggested. Better than standing here like a useless article, mulling over things that didn't bear thinking about. She walked to the bathroom and shut the door behind her...

'Not hungry?' Matthew pushed a rackful of toast towards Josie some fifteen minutes later. 'You really should try to eat something with your coffee. Food can do wonders for a hangover.'

'Do you have to keep going on about my hangover?' Josie had given this whole embarrassing situation a great deal of thought whilst standing under the spray, and had come to the conclusion that this situation—the situation that was so difficult for her—was far too easy and familiar for Matthew.

She felt vulnerable, that was the trouble, sitting across the round table from him with only a towelling robe separating Matthew from her nakedness. Not that he seemed remotely aware or perturbed by that fact—she clearly had as much sexual appeal as the toast he was persuading her to eat.

'I...I really don't think I can manage anything,' she murmured morosely. 'I...I'd rather just leave.' She wrapped the robe a little tighter around her bare legs. 'Matthew...' She closed her eyes for a moment and inhaled slowly to steady herself. 'About last night... I made such a fool of myself.'

'You had a bit too much to drink, that's all.' He lifted his broad shoulders in a shrug. 'It happens.'

'Not to me—at least not usually.' Josie frowned, forcing herself to continue. 'Look, you have to believe me,' she added hurriedly. 'I hardly ever drink. I hardly ever make a fool of myself...' She hesitated, peeping across at Matthew's gorgeous face from beneath lowered lids. 'How badly *did* I behave?'

'Not badly at all.' His gaze was direct. 'Foolishly, maybe—to drink so much wine—but...'

'I didn't...complain about being brought to your bedroom though, did I?'

'You were hardly in any state to complain.'

'Why didn't you take me home?'

He looked at her for a moment, studying the increased tension in her face. 'Because I don't know where you live,' Matthew replied carefully. 'Nothing happened, Josie,' he added tersely, 'if that's what you're worried about. I'm not in the habit of taking advantage of inebriated young women. I undressed you, and put you straight to bed. End of story.'

Josie felt the scorch of embarrassment flood her face. She should have kept her mouth shut! Oh, why hadn't she? Now she really did feel an absolute fool! 'Sorry! I wasn't... I mean I didn't expect or imagine that...' She forced a miserable smile and wondered what on earth Matthew must think of her. It was a wonder he didn't laugh out loud at the very idea that she thought they might have slept together. 'This hangover's definitely affected my brain!' Josie covered the burn in her cheeks with icy fingers and did her best to avoid his gaze. 'You've been very kind—'

'"Kind" had nothing to do with it.' Dark, enigmatic eyes gleamed suddenly. 'Believe me.' She felt totally confused in that moment, stilled by his look, by the sudden, almost husky tone of his voice. 'The pins are falling out of your hair,' he murmured.

'*What?*'

'The pins,' Matthew repeated. 'Here, let me...'

Her heart thudded wildly. He rose, and came around to her side of the table, began gently raking his fingers through the last vestiges of her once sophisticated chignon.

'Matthew—!' It was agonising, sitting still while his fingers roamed through her hair. Her scalp tingled, her body fizzed with a thousand and one sensations, all of them sending the same irrepressible message...

Foolish to do this. Foolish... Foolish...

Hell! What was the point in torturing himself this way? Being so close...allowing himself to be seduced by such fresh beauty, such irresistible sweetness. Where was his will-power? His *sense,* for goodness' sake? He thought of Josh and Abbie. Then after a moment willed himself to remember Kathryn.

He had made a promise—not the promise that she'd wanted, but a promise nevertheless. There was no room for a relationship in his life at the moment. He would try—try for the children's sake. No more bowing out, no more taking the easy option, no more running away. But Josie...

'That's all of them, I think.' Matthew moved from her suddenly, almost throwing the pins onto the table in front of Josie. 'You're right, your suit should be here by now,' he announced abruptly. 'I'll go down to Reception and find out what's happened to it.'

He left the room without another word. Josie listened to the click of the door. She sat at the table, as still and as rigid as when he had been close to her, wishing with all her heart that she could turn the clock back ten years, ten days, ten hours.

If she had known he would come back, maybe she could have prepared herself for his return.

She held her aching head. Then again...

What protection was there for a broken heart?

'I'd no idea this area had become so built up.' Matthew glanced at the row of identical recently erected houses as he drove. 'Neat, aren't they?'

'That's one way of putting it,' Josie replied dryly. 'As

far as I'm concerned they're characterless boxes. It's the next on the left, by the way,' she added quietly. 'Number twenty-two.'

'From that comment, I take it you're not particularly en-amoured.' Matthew flicked the indicator of his Jaguar and turned into her road. 'Why live here if that's the case? Couldn't you rent a flat or a house somewhere else?'

'Oh, it suits my purposes: relatively cheap, low mainte-nance.' Josie thought of Harcombe Hall—everything that her neat little box was not. 'Who wants to live in a rambling mansion anyhow?' she added bitterly. 'Draughty, horrible places!'

'At least you're a home-owner—not bad going for some-one in their mid-twenties. And before you bite my head off,' Matthew added swiftly, 'that was not meant to sound patronising.'

'No, I'm sure it wasn't…' Josie murmured vaguely. She didn't have the energy to take offence over trivia. She fixed her gaze out of the passenger window, thought about Matthew's bombshell from the night before—she wasn't sure she had the energy for anything any more…

He hadn't mentioned it again. And she hadn't asked—couldn't bring herself to. She was a coward. It was as sim-ple as that. He had found someone, someone he wanted to share his life with. He had a family. He had returned to settle down. She recited the facts silently in her head. Believe it! she told herself. That's it. Finished! The end of a dream—*two* dreams…

'It can be a pretty scary step owning your own home,' Matthew commented. 'Not everyone wants to commit themselves—especially when they're young.'

'At this moment in time I don't feel particularly young,' Josie murmured. 'More like a hundred years old, in fact. But then that's a hangover for you, I suppose.' She glanced at her house as the car pulled up outside and a wave of depression settled over her. 'Well, thanks for the lift!' She forced a smile, which practically cracked her face, and yanked open the car door.

Matthew caught hold of her arm just as she was about to get out. 'By the way,' he informed her. 'You haven't asked, but I arranged for your car to be taken to the local garage in town last night. I hope that's OK with you? They said they'd see to the punctures and have it ready for Monday morning.'

Her car. She hadn't asked because she had forgotten all about it. 'Oh…yes! Thank you very much. That was very kind of you.' She cringed inwardly. She sounded so polite, so awkward and ill at ease.

'Josie…!'

His hand was still on her arm, she could feel it scorching through the sleeve of her jacket. She raised dark lashes and looked into his face. 'Yes?' Her voice came out sounding somewhere between a croak and a whisper.

There was a pause. It lengthened. Finally he said, 'I'm sorry…for not being here for you after Sheila died.'

It wasn't what she had been expecting. 'Look…' Josie shook her head. 'I really shouldn't have said anything. It wasn't my place. I don't know what got into me.' She gave up trying to smile and showed him a closed, shuttered face instead. 'Let's just forget it all, shall we?'

Matthew removed his hand from her arm. 'If that's what you want,' he replied.

'It is. Very much.' Josie inhaled a breath. 'In fact, I'd like to forget all of it.' She forced another brief, awkward smile. 'My stupid singing, the disagreement we had in the wood. My tantrum outside…outside Har…that house,' she amended swiftly. 'Last night, this morning…' She paused momentarily. 'Everything.'

'Not exactly the best of beginnings, was it?' Matthew murmured.

'This isn't a beginning,' Josie announced. 'We…' She had been about to say that they'd known each other before, but 'known' wasn't a suitable word, and she couldn't think of another one, so she added, rather dramatically. 'It's the end.'

'What do you mean—the end?' The tone of his voice revealed mild amusement. 'End of what?'

'Of nothing,' Josie murmured.

Dark, unfathomable eyes watched her hurried exit from the car. She turned back, thought about saying something further, but after a glance at Matthew's stony expression she saw the futility of such a gesture. 'Goodbye,' she murmured with deliberate emphasis, and watched miserably as he thrust the car into gear and drove away.

Josie spent the rest of the morning trying to conjure up a positive frame of mind, but it was virtually impossible. There wasn't anything she wanted to do except sit and mope.

Even the simple task of turning on the flame-effect gas fire in her small sitting room caused misery, reminding Josie of Harcombe Hall. No pretend flames there, only the distinctive smell of wood burning brightly in the huge fireplaces. She had already foolishly planned to burn spruce in every fireplace at Christmas, for an added festive touch, so that the whole house would smell gloriously of fresh pine...

Josie wandered over to the phone and pressed the replay button on her answer-machine, listening whilst she retrieved her briefcase. She might as well try to do some work—submerging herself with business had been known to help in the past.

She optimistically spread papers over the coffee table and listened to the messages. One from Susan about work, reminding her that she had a meeting first thing Monday morning and needed to bring in some files with her, and one from Craig Taylor, her accountant. Josie listened to his commiserations about the loss of Harcombe Hall with a heavy heart. News travelled fast, she thought. But then Craig had his fingers in a lot of pies and had contact with an amazing amount of people. He sounded genuinely sympathetic, but it didn't help—nothing would.

Josie snapped the lid of her briefcase shut. She didn't want to think. What was the point? Matthew or Harcombe Hall. Both were lost to her. And there was nothing she could do about either of them.

She had been staring with unseeing eyes at the papers in front of her for an hour or so when the doorbell rang. Josie, startled out of her reverie, sat upright on the sofa in front of the fire, blinking rapidly. Who on earth could that be? Susan? She sometimes called by at the weekends, when Trevor, her fiancé was occupied with other things. Or Craig?

Please, not Craig, Josie thought blearily as she got up to answer the persistent ring. Her mind was as thick and lumpy as the packet of dried vegetable soup which had constituted her Sunday lunch; she didn't think she could cope with his post-mortem about Harcombe Hall just at this moment.

Josie walked through from the living room, glancing dejectedly in the hall mirror, pulling a face at the miserable, ghost-like reflection that stared back at her. Did she really want to answer the door? It wouldn't be anyone she could possibly want to speak to...

She peered through the spyhole and her heart leaped in her chest. It was. Matthew.

Josie stepped away as if electrified. Funny that after so many hours dwelling on him she should be thrown by his reappearance.

Her fingers fumbled with the catch and she opened the door. For several long seconds she forgot to breathe; all she could do was stare at him. He was leaning casually against the doorjamb, arms folded across his broad chest, dark hair flopping casually over one eye, wearing a well-worn sheepskin jacket which was surely doing a good job of keeping out the cold.

Josie finally remembered to gulp in some of the crisp,

raw air. 'Hello,' she murmured quietly. She would do this right, *play* it right, try and claw back at least some of her dignity. 'I didn't expect to see you again.'

'No.' Matthew's tone was enigmatic. 'You forgot your handbag.' He produced the neat patent leather item from behind his back and held it out to her. 'Clearly you haven't missed it.'

'No... I...' She frowned and took it from him.

There was an awkward pause—awkward as far as Josie was concerned anyway, though Matthew didn't seem in the least perturbed by the silence. After a long, assessing look at Josie's face, he eventually said, 'I'd like to go for a walk.'

'Oh?'

'With you.'

'Oh!' A bubble of excitement rose inexorably to the surface. Josie tried to push it back down, to remember what she had said earlier about there being an end to whatever there was between them—which was practically nothing, of course. Nothing at all.

'I'm not sure my legs have got the energy,' she murmured weakly.

'They will have.' He seemed very sure. 'Besides, you look as if you could do with the fresh air,' he asserted firmly, as Josie continued to stand in the doorway, mesmerised by the vision of him. 'Well, don't just stand there,' he added. 'Go put on your warmest coat.' He glanced up at the dull sky. 'The weather isn't as brilliant as yesterday, but I think we'll survive.'

It just felt right—to do as he instructed, to be with him. OK, so he had only returned because she had forgotten her handbag—she could live with that, and she could live with the brotherly smile. She could live with anything—just as long as she could spend some more time in his company...

'Come on in. I won't be a moment.' Josie held the door open wide as Matthew crowded into the small hallway.

He glanced through into the sitting room. 'You're working?'

'Oh, just a few bits and pieces.' Josie moved towards her briefcase and hastily began to bundle the papers one inside the other. 'I really wasn't in the mood anyway.'

'I don't mean to railroad you,' Matthew commented.

'You're not.' Josie thought about the past, tried very hard not to think about the future. Now. That was all she had. This moment. The pleasure of being with him. 'You're right about me needing some fresh air.'

'So where are we walking?' Josie asked as Matthew drove them both away from the estate, situated on the edge of town, in his sleek, brand-new Jaguar.

He glanced sideways and smiled. 'Wait and see.'

He drove in the direction of Harcombe village. After parking the car in a nearby lane, they began to follow one of the many footpaths which wound its way through the wood on the east side. But instead of continuing to the right when they reached a fork in the path, as Josie had expected, Matthew led the way to the left, and soon they were emerging from between the trees out onto a large, undulating meadow, where sheep grazed peaceably.

'Do you know, all these years and I had no idea there was a footpath through here?' Josie commented, glancing around her with interest. She frowned faintly. 'Actually, I'm not entirely sure where we are.'

'Tut! Tut! And you a native too!' Matthew's smile was totally infectious. 'Don't worry, I've got an ordnance survey map in my pocket. We won't get lost.'

I don't care if we do, Josie thought. Any time spent with Matthew felt like a bonus: precious hours and minutes before reality forced its ugly head.

She glanced up at the sky. It had an unexpectedly ominous look about it: whitish-grey and heavy, as if it were full of snow. She prayed silently that Matthew wouldn't notice and suggest they turn back.

'I wish I'd realised this was a public right of way,' she murmured. 'I'd like to come here in early summer—I should imagine this field's full of flowers then.'

'It's not.'

'What? Not full of flowers? How do you know?'

'I meant it's not a public right of way.'

'Oh!' Josie frowned in surprise. 'But that means...we're trespassing.'

'Don't look so horrified. Where's your sense of adventure?' Matthew's smile was alluringly playful. 'I had no idea you were such a law-abiding citizen!' He surveyed the sweep of field. 'You're right,' he murmured, suddenly serious. 'It will be beautiful in spring and summer.' He drew in a deep breath and surveyed the landscape. 'Newborn lambs, cowslips, primroses, bluebells... Funny how you don't really appreciate something until you've been parted from it.' His gaze when he turned to look at Josie was compelling. 'Coming back... For a while I wasn't sure if I was doing the right thing...'

'Why did you, then?' Josie's voice was quiet. She thought of the agony she would have to endure in the future, knowing he was around, catching sight of him...happy...settled...with someone else...

He lifted his broad shoulders in a shrug. 'Unfinished business, I suppose—the sense that I left this place too suddenly. I wanted to give it another chance—give myself one too...'

'Did it help—going away, I mean?' Josie's voice was very small. 'It must have...' She tried to make it easy for him—for them both. 'You were gone a long time.'

'I suppose it did—in the beginning at any rate. The excitement of new places, new people. It distracted me from the pain of Sheila's death. I pretended I was coping, of course, fooled myself into behaving a certain way, immersed myself in work, became successful...' His voice became brisk suddenly. 'Who knows? Certainly not me!' He flashed a heart-stopping smile, and Josie knew in an instant that that was all she was going to get. 'So, what about you?' Matthew's eyes narrowed as he contemplated her face. 'Ten years is a long time.'

'Yes, it is.'

'A lot can happen in that time.'

'Yes.'

'You don't want to tell me any of it?'

'What's to tell?' Josie averted her gaze. 'I've worked hard—only in an employment agency, of course, but it's kept the wolf from the door.'

'Ouch!' Matthew searched her face with a frown. 'Look, if I upset you, then I'm sorry. I just thought—'

'That I was capable of more,' Josie replied tartly. 'Yes, well, maybe I am,' she added. 'Maybe you jumped to a lot of conclusions and I've chosen not to enlighten you!'

'Really?' He chose to ignore the edge to her voice. 'Sounds interesting.'

She flashed him a frowning look. Should she tell him about her success now? Wouldn't it make all the difference? Wouldn't Matthew look at her in a new light—as a business woman, an equal, rather than the gauche schoolgirl he had left behind? *Wouldn't he be impressed?*

Josie hesitated, then made her decision. She was clutching at straws. Nothing she might say would change the fact that Matthew was lost to her. 'Not really,' she murmured. 'Not at all.' She inhaled sharply. 'Now, aren't we supposed to be walking?'

Matthew looked at her thoughtfully for a moment, then held out his hand. 'Absolutely. Come on, this way. There's something I want to show you.'

'Oh?' Josie stared at the strong, tanned fingers stretching out to take hers as if she were in a dream.

He tugged her towards him, holding her hand with smooth assurance, teasing her with a smile. 'You'll see when we get there.'

When the sleet and snow began to fall, it was not the gentle, picturesque flakes that Josie had secretly hoped for. The heavens opened like a trapdoor and they were engulfed in seconds.

'Goodness! This is amazing!' Josie announced, glancing up at the sky. 'Have you ever seen anything like it?'

'Bit of a freak storm. I know I've been in warmer climes recently, but this is a bit much for October, isn't it?'

'It's November in a couple of days' time,' Josie reminded him. 'There's no reason to suppose nature always has to check with the calendar!'

Within five minutes the ground was icy-white and the trees and hedgerows were difficult to define. The wind had whipped up, gusting the wet snow in fierce waves against their bodies as they crossed the field.

'Not so much a Christmas card, more like something from *Scott of the Antarctic!*' Matthew shouted. 'Are you all right? You should have worn a hat. Come on! Let's keep moving.'

He seemed to know exactly where he was heading—which was just as well, Josie thought, as she battled on, head down against the driving snow, for she had lost all sense of direction...

'Are you OK?' He pulled her to him after a while, bending his head so that his mouth was against her ear. She felt the warmth of his breath, longed to snuggle herself against the broad strength of his frame. 'It's not far now!'

'To where?' Josie asked, almost having to shout against the noise of the wind.

But Matthew didn't reply. He simply held her hand more tightly and continued to lead her through the ever deepening snow, which was already, Josie noticed, covering the laces of her boots.

It wasn't too long before Matthew halted again, putting an arm around her shoulders, pulling her chilled body close so that she could shelter against the warmth of his frame.

'Where are we?' Josie had absolutely no idea. For the last ten minutes or so she had kept her eyes virtually closed, allowing herself to be guided by Matthew as he led the way across first one field and then another.

'Take a look!' he instructed.

Josie narrowed her eyes against the snowflakes which were being battered into her face by the wind. For a while all she could see was snow, then, as her eyes adjusted to the conditions, she began to make something out...

Ahead, looming out of the swirl of whiteness, stood a large, impressive, all too familiar building.

Harcombe Hall.

CHAPTER FOUR

IT COULDN'T be. Josie gasped in surprise, then coughed as cold air and snow entered her gaping mouth. How could Matthew have brought her to Harcombe Hall without her realising?

More to the point, *why* had he brought her here? For what purpose?

She walked as if in a dream. She hadn't approached the house from this direction before. That was why, she supposed, she'd had no inkling of their eventual destination. If only she had paid more attention, been less absorbed with Matthew's proximity, she could have diverted the walk before it got this far...

'Did you *mean* us to come here?'

Matthew nodded and smiled, raising his voice, as Josie had done, above the sound of the wind. 'Yes, of course.'

'I thought...' She struggled, hanging onto the one possibility which would make everything if not all right then better. 'I thought perhaps you were as surprised to see it as I,' she replied hopelessly.

'It did seem to appear out of nowhere, didn't it?' Matthew glanced towards the house. 'Looks quite attractive from this distance, with the snow clinging to the wall.' His mouth curved. 'Hides all the defects.'

'Where are you going?'

It was a pointless question; she knew that. Josie shivered, watching as he began to climb over a battered stone wall, holding out a hand until Josie had done the same. He strode across a meadow which might conceivably once have been a manicured lawn, and Josie ran to catch up with him until they reached the south side of the building.

She brushed gloved fingers along the stone wall as she

went. She wished the house didn't still feel like a friend, didn't still mean something, but it did.

When reluctant legs brought her to the double front door, with its ornate but distinctly tarnished brass door knocker, Matthew was doing the one thing she'd dreaded—the one thing that Josie had spent a thousand hours dreaming about.

She watched with a sinking heart as he produced a large key from his pocket and inserted it into the lock. He pushed against the peeling front door, and it opened with creaking protest.

'Josie?' Matthew threw her a quizzical glance as he entered. 'What are you waiting for? Come inside before you freeze to death! *Josie?*' Dark brows drew together in a frown as she continued to stand outside in the snow. 'What on earth's the matter? You look as if you've seen a ghost!'

'I...' She shook her head helplessly.

His mouth curved into a meltingly attractive smile. 'It's not haunted, if that's what you're worried about. Come on!' Matthew held out his hand and tugged her towards the door. 'I want you to see it.'

'Matthew...' Words failed her. She could hardly believe this was happening. Josie crossed the threshold on legs that didn't feel as if they belonged to her. She glanced around the dimly lit hallway with a heart so heavy she was sure it must have turned to lead.

'At least it's dry in here,' Matthew commented. 'The survey did mention problems with the roof.' He glanced up at the blackened walls. 'But it seems to be holding out for the moment, at least in here.' He turned to Josie with a smile. 'What do you think?'

'About what?'

'The house, of course. Quite a monster, isn't it? I'm beginning to wonder if I haven't made one hell of a big mistake.' He crossed the hallway, glancing upwards, his feet echoing loudly on the ravaged stone floor. 'Every inch of sagging ceiling and crumbling piece of mortar reminds me of what lies ahead. Can you believe it?' he asked, in a voice which clearly indicated that he could scarcely believe it himself. 'This rambling old wreck is mine.' Matthew's amused announcement was tempered with a vague frown of anxiety. 'Tell me!' he murmured, dark eyes resting on her face in something approaching disbelief. 'Am I crazy, or am I *crazy?*'

'No. I...' Josie stared down at the floor, struggling to hold onto her composure. Oh, goodness, this was dreadful! How on earth was she supposed to handle this?

She wanted to cry: great racking sobs that would shake her whole body. Bad enough that Matthew wasn't ever going to be... Bad enough that. But Harcombe Hall taken from her as well?

'Josie?' She felt firm hands upon her shoulders, heard his deep voice close to her, full of concern. 'There is something the matter—what is it?' He tilted her chin with cool fingers. 'You look so pale.' He frowned down at her. 'Don't you feel well? Are you cold? Is that it?'

'Just a...a headache.' From somewhere Josie found the strength to look at him, to act as if she weren't desperate to throw herself into his arms and burst into floods of tears. 'I'm fine,' she added croakily, twisting her head away.

'You don't look fine. Come on.' Matthew put an arm around her shoulders. 'Let's go through here.'

The room was dusty and dirty, but even in its present state not without considerable charm. Once, a long, long time ago, it would have been an elegant drawing room.

Two well-proportioned windows flanked half-glazed French doors. Josie cast observant eyes over the peeling wood. The frames needed replacing. An expensive project, but one that was worth doing well. She had already, much to her chagrin, foolishly made enquiries with a firm that specialised in traditional methods of carpentry.

Unseeing eyes drifted to the jungle beyond the glass, almost pretty now, with its covering of snow. How many times had she designed the garden on scraps of paper? Ten? Twenty? She could see it all so clearly—a courtyard area near to the house, leading to the lawn, surrounded by exuberant herbaceous borders, neatly edged with box and lavender hedges...

'There's a stream down at the bottom of that far field,' Matthew murmured, coming to stand beside her. 'It's pretty rank at the moment, but once it's cleared of mud and debris it should be OK. I thought of creating a lake further up, maybe stocking it with fish...'

A lake. Josie hadn't thought of that. There was room. Yes, she thought miserably, a lake would be very nice...

'The weather looks set in. I had no idea it would be as bad as this. Sorry for dragging you out in this.'

'Sorry?' Josie threw him a narrowed glance, tried to focus on what he was saying. Matthew had stolen the house as well as her heart, and he was apologising for dragging her out in bad weather? She closed her eyes for a moment, clenching her hands into fists at her sides.

Something *was* wrong. He only had to look at her. She seemed edgy, tense, as if... She was regretting her decision to spend more time with him. She wanted to be somewhere else, *with* someone else. Dark eyes scanned her face, acknowledging the sudden change. He really couldn't think of any other reason for such a swift and marked alteration in her demeanour. Matthew cursed inwardly, annoyed with his own lack of understanding. *This was crazy.* What had seemed like a good idea at the time now felt crass and foolish...

Idiot, Jordan! Just because you feel compelled to spend time with her...

'I think I'd better leave.' Her voice, breathless and tense, cut through Matthew's silent curses, confirming what he had already thought.

'No, don't do that.' He regarded her steadily for a moment, before covering her clenched hands with his own. 'Come over here and get warm first.'

He led her gently to one end of the room, where the glow of an unexpected fire flickered in the large stone hearth. 'I took a chance,' he commented lightly. 'On the state of the chimney and on whether the fire would still be alight when we got here—I had no idea how long the wood would last.' Matthew removed a battered fireguard and drew a bemused Josie towards the flames. 'There's tons of wood lying around the estate,' he informed her. 'There'll be enough to burn in the house for the foreseeable future.'

'Yes...' Josie murmured quietly, trying not to think about the foreseeable future—a future which would see Matthew installed as owner. 'That will be...useful. You must be very...pleased.'

'It's one hell of an impulse buy, isn't it? I'm still trying to come to terms with the fact that I actually went through with it.'

'An *impulse buy*?'

Josie stared at Matthew's handsome profile in disbelief. Years of dreaming, months and months of planning and waiting, and...and Matthew had stepped in from out of the blue and bought it just on a *whim?* She closed her eyes tight, feeling the first surge of anger, sick with the unjustness of it all.

'Life has a certain ironic twist to it, don't you think?' Matthew continued, standing alongside her, staring down at the flames in thoughtful contemplation. 'Ten years ago I would have been disgusted at the idea of owning such a place—far too bourgeois. But here I am—a decade later—taking on a place like this...' He sounded different suddenly. Gone was the upbeat tone of a moment ago, in its place a voice, a look that held all sorts of unidentifiable emotion. 'And more...*much* more besides...'

Ironic? Josie thought. He could talk to her about *irony?*

'It's a large house for one. But of course...' Josie inhaled a steadying breath and forced steel into her voice. 'You aren't going to live here alone, are you?'

'No.' He glanced across at her, and his expression was difficult to read suddenly. 'No, I'm not.'

The cold reality of the situation flooded over her. How

could she bear it? Losing Harcombe Hall was bad enough—discovering she had lost it to Matthew...

He had bought this house for one reason and for one reason only. He had told her so himself, and now he had confirmed it once and for all. Why couldn't she just face the truth? Matthew was going to share this wonderful house with some lucky, lucky woman, and it wasn't going to be her.

She would never have Harcombe Hall; she would never have Matthew. This was the end.

'I can't stay here!' Josie wheeled away from him suddenly, and headed for the door. This was awful. *Awful!* She had to get away before she made an utter fool of herself and broke down completely.

She ran, literally ran, from one end of the room to the other, kicking up dust as she went, pushing aside a battered armchair, stumbling in her anxiety to get away from the one person, the one place that was causing her so much anguish.

'Josie!' Matthew, after his initial surprise, went after her. His feet thundered loudly on the bare wooden floor. He caught up with her in an instant. Josie felt the restraining presence of his hand on her arm and tried to shrug free of his hold, but his grip was firm and he turned her resolutely to face him. 'What on earth is the matter?'

'I told you.' Josie's voice was tight with emotion. 'I don't want to stay here.'

'Why?'

Josie looked into Matthew's wonderfully handsome face, struggling to hang onto her composure. 'Will you please let go of my arm?' she asked quietly.

He loosened his hold. Silence filled the room. 'Look, I know this place is a mess, but it's got to be better than—'

'You think I care about the mess? It's not that! I just can't stay!' Josie shook her head. 'I just can't,' she repeated shakily.

'For heaven's sake! Why not?' Dark, mesmeric eyes held

her gaze. 'Josie, we'll get ourselves warm and dry, wait until the snow eases up, and then we'll head back—'

'Don't tell me what to do!' Josie glared up at him, angry suddenly, hating his smouldering attraction and his sensible ideas, and the fact that he had got what she so desperately wanted—*was* what she so desperately wanted. 'If I want to leave now, then I will!'

Matthew looked into her face for a long moment, clearly struggling to comprehend the reason for her sudden vehemence. 'What is it? What's bothering you?' His voice was vibrant with compassion. 'Tell me!'

'No!' Josie hated the reasonable tone of his voice, the caring look in his eyes. Why couldn't he lose his temper as she wanted him to? Then it would be easy to walk away. 'Nothing!' she flared. 'Absolutely nothing!'

'This is *nothing?*'

'Why did you buy this place?' she asked fiercely. *'Why?'*

Dark eyes narrowed. 'Because I wanted it,' he replied calmly.

'As simple as that!' Josie couldn't keep the bitterness from her voice. 'You must be very wealthy,' she added miserably. 'To be able to throw so much money away on a whim!'

'Look, I realise draughty, ramshackle old houses aren't your thing, but I really wanted to share this with you.' His voice was steel-edged now. 'This is a big step for me—'

'You think I *care* about that?' Josie shook her head in disbelief. In that moment she hated him—hated him for not understanding, for reappearing out of the blue and putting her through all of this. 'Share it with your woman! Not with me!' she cried. 'I'm nothing! A nobody! Just a failed grade-A student with a foolish inclination to get inebriated every once in a while!'

Trembling, cold fingers reached for the dull brass handle, but Matthew banged the door shut out of her grasp. Stunning dark eyes glinted dangerously. 'Don't talk like that,' he commanded.

'Why not?' Josie gulped a breath, hardly able to look

into his face. 'It's the truth—or what you perceive to be the truth!' she added bitterly. 'I can't believe you thought I would be interested in this wreck of a house—or in you, or...or in anything you might do!'

'Oh, no?' He pulled her close suddenly. She could feel the muscular line of his thigh pressing against her body, was aware of the glint in his eyes, recognised the danger of such blatant confrontation, but only when it was too late—much, much too late. 'I'll show you the truth,' he gritted huskily. 'This is the truth...'

He lowered his head and his mouth closed over hers. It wasn't gentle, or romantic—none of the things Josie had spent her teenage years fantasising about. Their first kiss was harsh and angry and passionate, taking her breath away, causing her to stagger under the onslaught, so that she would have sunk to the floor in a faint if Matthew hadn't have been holding her so tightly.

Josie had never experienced anything like it. *Never.* She couldn't think; she couldn't breathe. Just exist. Far out on another planet, reeling under the intoxicating advance.

And it *was* intoxicating—a quick-acting, very powerful drug. Capable of altering her senses, of bending her will. Even when Matthew chose to change the tempo she found she was still under his spell. Mesmerised, awed by a kiss that was urgent, sensual, by the softness of a caress which found her pressing against him, lifting her own hesitant hands to touch the broad line of his shoulders, the nape of his neck...

She had never been held or kissed like this before, as if she was cool, fresh water and he was a man dying of thirst...

He could scarcely believe this was happening—that he had instigated this moment. *Crazy...crazy...* But he didn't seem able to come to his senses. He loved the taste of her, the touch of her, every heart-stopping second of being this close to her...

He didn't want to have to think about the worries of the future, just the glory of this precious, neverending moment. He wanted to hold her close and never let her go…

A spark from the flames, reverberating like gunshot around the empty room, shocked both of them to their senses.

Josie felt cruelly cheated as Matthew dragged his mouth away from hers, as the cold reality of what had taken place between them flooded through her. She watched as he searched her face with a frown. Still holding her, still close. Dark head bent over hers. She could feel the warmth of his breath on her cheek, see the way his chest was rising and falling in unison with hers. 'Josie—'

'*Don't!*' Her voice was as cold and icy as the storm which was swirling and howling around the house. 'Just don't say a word!' she said wildly, pulling violently away. 'I don't want to hear anything you might have to say to try and justify—'

'*Justify?*' He stood still, dark, smouldering eyes watching her. It was very quiet now, with only the crackle and hiss of the fire and the thudding of Josie's heart to be heard. 'Is that what you think I should do?'

She showed him a glassy, shuttered face. 'I don't care what you do!' she flared. 'You were angry. So was I. That's all there was to it!'

'You know that's not true.'

'I want to leave!' Josie's voice was hard and unforgiving, hiding a welter of emotion.

'Josie…!' Matthew's expression was ominously fierce. He searched her face with a frown. 'We need to talk.'

'No, we don't. *I* don't want to.' Josie's eyes filled with tears. 'Wrong time, wrong place…' She hesitated, willing herself to say it, knowing that if she wanted this to be over cleanly, quickly, then she had to go through with it. 'Wrong person,' she added with an anguished glance. 'It happens.'

'I see.'

It was difficult to keep the bitterness from his voice. How could he have done this? How could he have acted so…so foolishly? Her expression afterwards—so shocked, so full of hate...

'I'll walk you back.'

'I can go on my own!'

'If you think I'm letting you go out alone, when the weather's as bad as it is—!' he growled.

'OK! OK!' Josie held her hands up in a gesture of defeat, and backed away. 'I just want to get out of here,' she cried. 'Why are you making everything so difficult for me?'

She was being unfair—*so* unfair. Josie marvelled at Matthew's ability to keep cool. The things she had said to him... Well, this was it—the end. A friendship over before it had begun—if indeed it had ever been friendship...

He didn't attempt to talk or to touch her during their walk back to civilisation. It was best that way. There was no way of changing things, not now—too much had been said, and all of it by her.

Josie shook her head in despair as she plodded through the snow, which was too wet and already melting fast, conscious of Matthew's overwhelming presence a few feet away. He seemed locked in another world anyway. What was he feeling? she wondered. Guilt? Regret? Both those things and more besides, if the grave expression on his face was anything to go by.

Dislike and disgust just about summed it up, Josie decided.

She stood awkwardly, once they'd reached the parked car, watching as Matthew searched for his keys in the pocket of his jacket. He looked so magnificent, but so unapproachable too; there was a hard, grim line to his mouth, a tightness along his jawline which indicated only too well the way he was feeling.

She stared at the low, sleek sports car in dismay. She didn't think she could bear the agony of a ride home in such confined surroundings.

'Josie!' She turned sharply at the sound of her name,

looking across to where a shiny hatchback had drawn to a careful halt on the other side of the road.

'Susan!' Josie didn't think she had ever been so pleased to see her friend and secretary.

She watched as the rotund figure, dressed warmly in a fake fur coat, got out of the car and crossed the sleety road with cautious steps.

'Isn't this weather just dreadful?' Susan huddled inside her coat, smiled at Josie, and then threw an obviously interested glance in Matthew's direction. 'You two are brave. Been for a walk, have you?'

'Yes, we got caught in the storm,' Josie replied breathlessly. 'This is Matthew,' she announced swiftly, before Susan could come out with some witty or not so witty remark. 'Matthew...' She glanced into his shuttered face and then quickly away again. 'This is Susan. We...work together.'

Matthew took Susan's hand courteously, but his smile was brief and distracted. 'Hello, Susan. Pleased to meet you.'

'Likewise, I'm sure!' Susan eyes lingered on Matthew's handsome face for a long moment, although he himself seemed oblivious to her assessing gaze.

'Are you driving back to town?' Josie asked, anxious to terminate the awkward situation as quickly as possible.

'Yes, just been over at my folks for lunch. I could do with a long lie-down. I ate too much, as usual.'

'Could I...?' Josie's voice cracked fractionally. 'Could I cadge a lift, do you think?'

'What—from me?' Susan didn't bother to hide her surprise. 'Of course,' she added. 'If you're sure you want to ride in my car. The inside looks as if a bomb has hit it, mind you.'

'So what's new?' Josie tried to smile, but it was impossible. She lowered her head, stared at her sodden leather boots, wriggled toes that were past any feeling, and wished her heart could be the same.

Matthew turned, regarding Josie in formidable silence for

a moment. 'I can give you a lift back home,' he informed her evenly. 'It's no trouble.'

It took an effort of will to keep her voice steady, but she managed it—somehow. 'No...thank you anyway,' she added, conscious of Susan's presence. 'Your hotel's in the opposite direction, and as Susan has to drive past my house...' Josie inhaled a deep breath. 'I really would prefer to drive back with Susan.'

There was a moment of silence. 'If that's what you want,' Matthew replied coolly.

'It is.' Josie met his dark gaze.

'Goodbye, then.'

There was an awkward moment, when neither of them moved. Then Matthew held out his hand, and after a slight pause Josie placed her fingers in his. Feeling the strength and warmth of him, fighting against the shock of awareness which travelled through her body like a bolt of brilliant white lightning, was difficult to say the least. Ebony eyes scorched her face, almost destroying what little composure she had left.

'Look after yourself,' Matthew told her quietly.

It was a farewell. That much was obvious. She nearly broke then, nearly threw herself into his arms to beg forgiveness. Only the presence of Susan prevented Josie from making a complete and utter fool of herself.

'You too,' Josie murmured.

A strange, almost dangerous stillness settled over the two of them, then Matthew turned abruptly, opened his car door and got in without another word.

'Wow!' Susan's voice was rich, first with admiration, then with scorn, as the two women stood side by side and watched the sleek Jaguar pull away. 'I cannot believe you have just passed up the opportunity to spend more time with a man as gorgeous as that! What have you done— given pleasure up for Lent? And what's all this about me having to go past your house? I live in the opposite direction.'

'Let's just get in the car, shall we, Susan?' Josie murmured wearily as she began to cross the road. 'My feet are freezing.'

Winter. Not the best of times for feeling low and miserable and lonely. The weeks had passed slowly. Working hard at the office seemed to make little difference. The employment agency was opening another branch in a town a few miles away, which meant a lot of organising and travelling to oversee the operation, but even with this extra interest Josie still managed to find time to dwell on Matthew, and Harcombe Hall, and the awful mess she had somehow managed to make of everything.

Josie rose from her desk and walked to the window. Outside, on this grey December morning, the whole world was going about its business. The bustle in the high street was proof that the countdown to Christmas had begun in earnest. Josie's eyes drifted along the line of shops, crammed with gaudy decorations and eye-catching goods.

Any other year and she would have felt at least a little interested; now it was almost impossible not to feel depressed by it all.

'Here are the files you wanted.' Susan, bright and breezy as ever, burst into Josie's small, but well-appointed office and dropped the folder she was carrying onto her desk. 'Latest recruits! I had a quick look through them and they do look OK.' She grinned. 'I might even want to employ some of them.'

'Good.'

'Anything else?' Susan asked. 'Only I've got masses of typing to get through...'

'No...no, that's fine,' Josie murmured.

Susan, dressed in a seasonally vibrant suit of red, which should have clashed horribly with her bubble of auburn hair but somehow didn't, came and stood beside her at the window. 'Christmas soon!' she announced cheerfully. 'I'm beginning to get that excited, tingling feeling already, aren't you?'

'Mmm...'

Josie didn't think she could stand it. She thought about the prospect of yet another festive season spent alone—or, if not entirely alone, then at least without someone special to share it with. She thought of the usual get-together she had with similarly placed friends. It really didn't appeal this year: giving presents that had been difficult to think of and a nightmare to buy, dining out, pretending they were all having a whale of a time when she knew that if they were honest each and every one of them was simply making the best of a bad job—just like herself.

I want a family! Josie cried silently.

Perhaps she should try and get away. These last few weeks had been a living nightmare: always thinking about him, remembering every look, however innocent, the touches that weren't, longing to lay eyes on him, frightened that she would...

The traffic was horrendous. It was a Wednesday, and a market day, and that made the queue for the lights outside the offices particularly lengthy. Josie watched as an impatient man in a pristine vehicle made angry gestures at a rather absent-minded old lady who seemed to be having trouble with her gears.

'Doesn't look like he's heard of the season of good will,' Susan remarked. 'Where's the silly old fool's Christmas spirit? Look, he's making her even more flustered by hooting his horn at her.'

Josie glanced at the elderly lady driver, then her gaze drifted along the line of cars. Later she would wonder what had made her dwell on that particular vehicle, for there had been no apparent reason, except maybe the children—so appealing in their matching hats and coats, their olive-skinned faces full of innocent excitement...

The sturdy four-wheel drive vehicle edged forward in the queue of traffic. Parcels and foil-wrapped presents were piled up behind and the two smiling children, wrapped up against the cold, could just be seen through steamed-up windows, laughing and chatting with their parents in front.

The female passenger of the maroon Range Rover wound

down her window, turned back to speak to the children behind, and in that moment the driver of the vehicle became visible.

Josie's heart leapt. He looked the same, only more handsome, if that were possible—more tanned, more happy, more *everything*. Laughing at something, turning his dark head towards the beautiful woman sitting beside him—and she *was* beautiful, incredibly so, possessing the same olive skin as her children, a good profile and long dark hair—looking into her face, returning her smile, *loving her*.

They were a family. Josie's gaze was dragged, spellbound, towards the children sitting on the back seat of the Range Rover. A boy and a girl of about eight and six, carbon copies of their parents—*adorable*.

It was torture, but she watched for as long as they were there, mesmerised by the sight of them, feeling worse than she had ever thought she would now that the vision of Matthew and his family was a solid, indisputable fact.

He didn't see her watching him. That was the only thing she could draw comfort from. Besides, he was too engrossed in his loved ones to be distracted by Josie's rigid figure, staring at him through an insignificant office window.

The traffic lights changed. Susan said something, but Josie didn't hear what it was. Every ounce of concentration, every thought, was still fixed on the vehicle and its occupants, long, long after it had moved out of sight.

'Wasn't that—?'

Josie met Susan's narrowed gaze. 'Yes.' She sprang away from the window, feeling a wave of heat rushing over her. Josie placed a trembling hand to her forehead and realised she felt unexpectedly nauseous.

'Josie?' Susan looked up into her face and placed a hand on her arm. 'You look awful. What is it? Are you unwell?'

'No. No. I'm all right.' Josie found to her horror that tears were welling up in her eyes. Hastily she reached towards the box of tissues on her desk. 'Sorry,' she murmured, wiping her eyes. 'I don't know what's come over me.'

'There's no need to apologise.' Susan looked on with genuine sympathy. 'If I can help…?

Josie shook her head. 'There's nothing to do.'

'Was it…?' Susan hesitated a moment. 'They may just have been good friends.'

Josie let out a sigh. 'No,' she replied. 'No, they're not just good friends.'

'Oh, I see. I thought you'd been pretty quiet about him recently. Oh, you poor thing! It's horrible when your private life is in a mess.' Susan placed an arm around Josie's shoulders. 'I should know,' she added, pulling a wry face, 'having Trevor as a fiancé. You've really got it bad, haven't you?'

Josie managed a weak smile. 'I didn't realise I was such an open book,' she murmured, wiping her eyes.

'Ah, well, the signs are there—and we've been together for a few years now, haven't we?' Susan replied. 'Even at typing class on a Monday evening I used to be able to judge whether you'd had a good weekend at home. You know,' she added a little awkwardly, 'with your mum and dad arguing like they did. So, you and…?'

Josie heaved a steadying breath. 'Matthew.'

'You and he have had problems?'

'Sort of.'

Susan shook her head. 'Meaning?'

'Meaning…' Josie began tremulously. 'Meaning that I have got it bad, but I shouldn't have. He's not mine now. He never has been mine, nor will he ever be…'

'Unrequited love?' Susan sighed. 'Oh, that's awful!'

Josie tried her best to be upbeat. 'And at my age too!' She held up a warning hand as Susan opened her mouth again. 'Look…I know you mean well, Susan, but I really don't want to talk about it.'

'Not ever?'

'Well, not now, that's for sure,' Josie replied miserably. 'I can't…'

'Trevor's out quite a few evenings now—if you ever want to come round...'

'How is dear Trevor?' Josie made a huge effort and smiled brightly, determined to change the subject. 'Still working all the hours God sends?'

'You two would make a good pair!' Susan commented. 'And, yes, he is. Started another evening class—and takes on all the overtime he can get.'

'I'm surprised you get a chance to see each other,' Josie commented distractedly, 'with the amount of part-time study he undertakes.'

'We don't—well, hardly. And it's going to be even worse soon. The firm Trev works for has been asked to work up at that big house—you know, the one on the edge of town that's being renovated. They must have every builder within a twenty-mile radius working on that place—'

'You mean Harcombe Hall?' Josie had to concentrate very hard to keep her voice level.

'Yes, that's it! Trevor had a quick look around last week. He says it's going to be lovely when it's finished. The roof's been fixed, but parts of the interior have had to be virtually gutted and built all over again—new ceilings, walls, floors, that sort of thing.'

Josie gulped a breath. 'And...and does Trevor know when the family are moving in?'

'Soon, I think.' Susan, always active, was collecting the post to go from Josie's 'out' tray. 'One wing of the house has been made ready earlier than the rest. Trev says he's quite looking forward to wielding his paintbrush. There are some lovely fancy bits of moulding.' Susan, smiling, glanced across, then frowned at Josie's tortured expression. 'What's the matter? Oh, no, that's not where—?'

'Yes.' Josie nodded, thankful that apart from everything else Susan didn't know about her failed attempt to buy the place—she didn't think she could cope with more sympathy. 'Yes, it is.'

There was a knock at the office door. Josie inhaled a

steadying breath. 'Come in!' A young girl with neat features and shiny hair stuck her head round the door. 'Yes, Cathy, what is it?'

'Sorry to interrupt Miss James, but it's a bit busy out here. We wondered if Susan could come out and give a hand.'

'It's OK. I'll do it!' Josie rose from behind her desk, glad of the opportunity to be distracted. 'I'm not in the mood for any of this at the moment.' She glanced down at the mass of paperwork scattered over her desk, then across at Susan. 'Thanks for caring, Susan,' she whispered as she passed. 'It means a lot to me, honestly.'

She breezed through into the smart outer office, decorated in red and green, blocking out anything and everything except the concerns of work. It was unexpectedly busy, but then that was often the way things went. Josie smiled at Marilyn, her oldest employee, who was dealing with a familiar client, noted that Dawn didn't appear to have the correct company blouse on once again, and then proceeded to the waiting area, which was attractively screened from the main office by a few astronomically priced large plants and painted wrought-ironwork.

They were face to face before there was time to back out. Josie felt the heat rush to her face.

The awfulness of it.

The horror of discovering that the agency's latest client was none other than Matthew's beautiful lover.

CHAPTER FIVE

FOR a long moment Josie could do nothing except stare. A vision of Matthew and this beauty—laughing, loving, intimate together at Harcombe Hall—clouded her vision.

She was dressed casually: grey woollen slacks and black cashmere pull-over clothing a slender figure. Discreet make-up, dark hair pulled back into a simple ponytail. Perfect.

Josie opened her mouth to speak, but no words appeared. She tried again, noting the arched brows, the faint look of disdain, forcing herself to operate on automatic pilot until the shock of this first meeting could die down. But it showed no sign of doing that. She felt weak, as if something unexpectedly heavy had cannoned into her. She found her voice—just—although the usually smooth and friendly welcome came out sounding awkward and hesitant. 'Good...morning. Would you...like to come this way, please?'

Josie walked on shaking legs to a vacant desk in the main office, and gestured to the seat opposite her own. She glanced around the office and saw, with a sinking heart, that everyone else was still busy.

'How can I help you?'

'I need staff.'

'I see.' Josie rifled through the desk drawer, looking for the correct form, although in truth she knew exactly where everything was.

'A housekeeper and a nanny, and a cleaner—someone who comes in two, maybe three times a week. We've just moved into the area—Harcombe Hall.' A smile from the immaculately painted mouth: brief, automatic, superior. 'You might know the place.'

'Er...y-yes.' Josie, avoiding the woman's gaze, which

75

seemed altogether too assessing, gulped a breath and busied herself with selecting a pen from the holder on the desk. 'A…very nice house—or so I believe,' she added quickly.

'Well, it will be—one day. Although when that day will be…' The beautiful woman continued, leaning back in her chair, crossing one long leg elegantly over the other, 'Everything's in such a mess at the moment—dust and builders all over the place. We have two children,' she added mercilessly. 'The nanny especially will have to be experienced. They need…' She hesitated, searching for suitable words. 'Careful handling.'

'I see.' Josie kept her gaze fixed to the form on the desk in front of her.

'How quickly will you be able to supply the right people? In time for Christmas? Only, as you can imagine, I have a lot on my plate at the moment, and the last thing I need is more chaos in the house. The builders have been practically living alongside us. I had no idea…no idea that it would be like this at all!' The dark head shook reflectively. 'So you can see my position?' she added, after a moment, piercing Josie with beautiful almond-shaped eyes. 'It's vital we have help as soon as possible. My…' there was a slight hesitation '…partner and I need to have more time to ourselves.' Josie was subjected to a brief, but incredibly attractive smile, which intimated far more than she ever wanted to know. 'Our relationship is immensely important to both of us.'

And what about your relationship with your children? Josie wondered silently. Isn't that important too?

'The agency will certainly do its best,' Josie murmured. 'Once I've completed the details, we'll select from the employees on our files and you'll be able to interview—'

'Oh, good! You will call me as soon as you find someone, won't you?' The young woman rose swiftly, an exotic beauty towering above Josie's seated figure. 'Presumably I can safely leave the agency to deal with everything? Only, as you can imagine, I'm incredibly busy at the moment. I have masses of other things to deal with.'

'But there are a few more details yet,' Josie replied, taken aback by the brevity of the consultation. Most clients were prepared—indeed wanted—to make sure they had covered absolutely everything. 'Hours of work, details of pay structure... I don't have the ages of your children,' Josie added swiftly, glancing down at the paper on the desk.

'Live-in housekeeper, live-in nanny, and—oh, I don't know...' The slender shoulders were lifted in a slight shrug, 'The cleaner to come in three or four times a week. We're willing to pay the going rate, of course, and as to the ages of the children, they're seven and five. You will call as soon as you come up with anything, won't you? Only, as I've already indicated, it is extremely urgent that we get staff.' She cast Josie and the office a calculating glance. 'This agency *is* up to the task, I take it? I've made enquiries and heard good reports, but if you don't think you can handle our requirements—'

Josie stood up finally. 'Oh, we can handle them, Ms...' Her eyes were drawn to the gold band on the third finger of the woman's left hand, and she felt, much to her own horror, her eyes pricking with tears. She inhaled a sharp breath. 'If the agency could have your telephone number, so that we can contact you?'

'Oh, yes, of course!'

Josie watched the smooth, elegant hand, with its painted nails in deepest burgundy, reach for pen and paper, and tried not to dwell on the fact that of all the hands in all the world these were the ones that mattered most to Matthew— that this woman was his woman, his love, his wife, the mother of his children.

'There we are!' The immaculately manicured fingers handed Josie the piece of paper, then picked up the gilt-edged handbag from the desk. There was a flash of perfect white teeth. 'I hope to hear from you shortly. You did make a note of my address, didn't you?' she added unnecessarily. 'Harcombe Hall.'

'Harcombe Hall. Yes,' Josie replied stiltedly, glancing

down at the paper in her hand, the flourish of a name—Kathryn Jordan—beside the telephone number.

How could she ever forget?

It was inevitable that she should feel compelled to look at the house.

Seeing him again had been the catalyst—seeing *them.*

All things considered, Josie felt that in the circumstances she had done very well to keep away as long as she had. The previous month or so had felt more like years, and besides, after this morning…well, she only had so much will-power.

Josie refolded the ordnance survey map and stuffed it into the pocket of her chunky cardigan. She had her route planned down to the last centimetre. Just a gentle meander—after all, she loved walking, didn't she? And she needed the fresh air. And there was no reason *why* she shouldn't change her routine from time to time.

To say that Susan had been surprised at Josie's announcement that she was going to take the rest of the day off…

Josie shook her head. She was dressed in her scruffiest clothes: faded denims, white tee-shirt, and a thick navy cardigan that had definitely seen better days—more to prove a point than for any practical reason, as a sort of personal reassurance. For she was here only to catch a glimpse of the house, to see what had been done to her beloved Harcombe Hall, not for any other reason. OK, so she was acting out of character. Most people did that at one time or another, didn't they?

She had brought her binoculars with her, and that made her feel uneasy, as if she were some kind of spy or something, when the truth was she often brought them along with her on walks. *She really did.* Of course, she might just raise them to her eyes and scan along the line of the roof, see what sort of job had been done on it—Susan had said Trevor thought it pretty good, but she would just like to check for herself…

Late morning, and the day was dry and blustery, with patches of blue sky appearing occasionally through clouds that had hung low and heavy for the last three days.

Josie walked briskly, doing her best to ignore her thudding heart, trying to concentrate on her surroundings. It was difficult. Her mind kept reliving the scene that morning when she had come face to face with Matthew's...with the beautiful Mrs Jordan.

She wondered how Susan was doing; finding suitable employees for Kathryn Jordan was surely going to prove to be a problem, especially this close to Christmas. The agency had very high standards, and Josie had her suspicions that any housekeeper, or indeed any nanny worth their salt would certainly not be available at such short notice. Not that Matthew's wife seemed particularly worried about quality, she thought. She seemed simply keen to fill the void in time for the festive season, so that she and Matthew could spend lots of precious time together...

Josie closed her eyes tightly for an agonised moment. She mustn't think about that—about them. She just wanted to look at the house, that was all. Just the house...

It was easy to feel reasonably confident whilst she was under cover, but when the moment arrived to change course, to emerge from under the shelter of trees and make a break for open countryside, she hesitated, as she had always known she would, and wondered for the fiftieth time if she were doing the right thing.

Josie slowed her pace after negotiating first one field, then another, conscious of the shortening distance between herself and Harcombe Hall. She was just metres from the surrounding land, only a hedge and a tumbling dry brick wall between her and trespassing.

There was the house. Josie positioned herself behind a hedge and looked at the building with affection. It seemed vastly improved, even from this distance; the brickwork had been cleaned, and it had already lost its uncared for appearance.

Josie raised the binoculars to her eyes and surveyed the

new roof and window-frames. A good job done. She released a sigh and was glad. At least the old place was getting the attention it deserved. The interior would be the absolute test, of course, but there would be little chance of ever viewing that—not that she thought she could bear to anyway...

The high-pitched sound of children's voices made Josie start, and scurry back to avoid detection. She hadn't imagined anyone would be out and about this far from the house.

She gave her heart a moment to stop thumping and then peered cautiously over the brambles. The chatter came from the other side of the hedge, somewhere below, to her left. She looked again. The two children were playing beside the stream. Dressed in red and blue wellington boots, with dungarees and rainbow jumpers, intent on some self-appointed task, chatting to each other with serious expression as they moved stones and old pieces of wood.

Josie frowned, conscious of the danger of their play as the elder child, the boy, slipped down the bank and splashed, thankfully feet first, into the stagnant water. She shook her head. The stream looked deep in places. Deeper than was safe, surely, for two children of their ages to be left unattended?

For that was definitely how it looked. Josie surveyed the area, scanning the fields between herself and the house, peering cautiously this way and that, confirming that there seemed to be no sign of either parent.

There was a sudden scream, then another. Josie's heart leapt in her chest. Without stopping to think of anything but the worst, she scrambled around the shelter the bramble hedge afforded, vaulted the stone wall and ran down the incline towards the children...

The young boy had wonderful dark eyes. He looked at her now in surprise, and all Josie could think of was Matthew.

'Who are you?' His gaze was large and direct and totally disarming.

'I'm— Where's your sister?' Josie asked urgently.

The boy frowned. There was another high-pitched scream. Mistake, Josie thought, as she followed the sound with her eyes, as a sharp stab of awareness scorched through her body, as her hands shook and she halted unsteadily on her feet.

Big mistake. The strength of her reaction at seeing him was so strong it surprised even Josie. He took her breath away. Even that first meeting—all those weeks ago now—hadn't left her feeling like this…so…mesmerised…captivated by the sight of him. She wasn't able to run, or hide or do any other remotely sensible thing. Just stand and stare, wondering how she was ever going to find the strength to live without him.

He looked wonderful, dressed in old denims and a thick plaid shirt, his dark hair falling over one eye, tanned, healthy, smiling. Josie's heart flipped over in her chest. A happy father, playing with his children…

'*Josie?*' Matthew stopped swinging his daughter through the air and looked at her in astonishment. 'What are you doing here?'

It was as if he had conjured her up out of his imagination. Could he be hallucinating? He wasn't, of course. She was there, standing before him with that faintly vulnerable expression, large blue eyes wide with discomfort. Looking just as gorgeous as he remembered…

Now what was she supposed to say? Three pairs of dark eyes surveyed her with open curiosity. Josie longed to have the soggy ground she was standing on open up and swallow her whole.

'I…I was just passing. I heard the screams and…' She halted, aware of the foolishness of her explanation.

'Just passing?' Matthew strode towards her, carrying the little girl under his arm like a roll of carpet. From the giggling and the gleeful expression on the rosy-cheeked face, she clearly loved every minute of it.

'I was just…walking.' Josie thrust her hands awkwardly

into the pockets of her cardigan and felt the coldness of the binoculars against her fingers. 'I...I didn't mean to interrupt. Sorry, my mistake!' She attempted a smile, but it faltered into little more than a miserable grimace. 'I'll leave. Foolish of me to think...sorry,' she repeated awkwardly, and began to turn away. 'Sorry—!'

'Hey!' Matthew caught her arm. 'Stop apologising, will you? It's good to see you, whatever the reason.' Stunning eyes regarded her flushed face for a moment. 'Let me introduce you,' he added smoothly. He gestured to the boy, who came over—somewhat reluctantly, Josie felt—and ruffled his mop of dark curly hair with an affectionate hand. 'This is Josh. Josh, this is Josie.' A warm smile tugged the corners of his mouth. 'A vaulter supreme. Did you see the way she cleared that wall? Clearly someone who can be relied on in a crisis.'

'Even when there isn't one!' Josie avoided Matthew's gaze, and gave the boy a rueful smile. 'Hello, Josh. It's nice to meet you. I hope I didn't give you too much of a fright, springing from nowhere like that.'

The boy lifted his shoulders in a shrug. 'No, it's OK. It was something different. I was pretty bored anyway.'

'Oh.' Josie glanced across at Matthew, who was, she saw, staring at Josh in frowning contemplation.

'And now Abbie!' Matthew's dark, attractive voice lifted with determined cheerfulness. 'Where is she?' He spun around, and there was a squeal of delight from beneath his arm. 'Josh? Have you seen Abbie? She was here earlier—'

'Stop! Stop! I'm here! I'm here!'

'Where?' He swung round again, causing more giggles. 'Daddy!'

Daddy. It was like a dagger in Josie's heart. *Daddy...*

Matthew laughed and set his daughter on her feet. 'This is Abbie, and she is a handful, as you may or may not have gathered! Abbie, say hello to Josie.'

The little girl held out a hand in formal manner. Josie bent down and took the dainty fingers, regarding the suddenly solemn expression with a smile. 'Hello, Abbie.'

'Do you want to play with us? We're seeing if there are any fish in the stream. Look! We've got nets!' She stomped in her red wellington boots to where they lay and picked them up triumphantly.

'And have you caught anything?' Josie directed her question at Josh, conscious that the boy needed to be included.

'No, only slime and mud. It was a pretty stupid idea anyway.' He scuffed the ground with the toe of his boot. 'This stream isn't any good.'

'Oh, but one day it will be, won't it?' Josie moved towards the edge of the bank to inspect the barely flowing water below. 'It just needs clearing out, then you can stock it with fish, maybe build a bridge across. Do you know that game? The one where you float a stick in the water and race it against another? You'll be able to do that.'

'Like in *Winnie the Pooh?*' Josh asked, frowning a little.

'Exactly like that!'

'I love Winnie the Pooh!' Abbie began jumping up and down excitedly. 'Daddy has started reading us all his stories at bedtime!'

'Has he?' Josie tried to smile, but the sudden vision of Matthew reading with the children, freshly washed and dressed in their pyjamas, rose before her, and in a flash she saw the folly of her presence, the danger of being captivated by the children. By him. 'That's nice.' She hesitated, then forced herself to sound cheerful and full of fun. 'Well, it's been a pleasure to meet you both, but I'd better leave you to your stream-clearing!'

She risked a quick glance at Matthew, blushed at the all-seeing, all-smouldering gaze, and turned from him, from them all, wondering how on earth she would ever find the will-power to walk away.

'*Josie!*' Matthew fell into step alongside. He shook his head, throwing her a good-humoured frown. 'Not a chance!'

'What?'

She watched as he considered her frantic expression carefully. 'You think we're going to allow you to leave, just like that? Come inside—have a cup of coffee.'

'I don't drink coffee...'

His mouth curved into a smile. 'Tea, then—hot chocolate, whisky, vodka.' His voice lowered suddenly, dark eyes intent. 'Anything...'

Josie looked back at Josh and Abbie, who were chasing each other with soggy nets. 'They're lovely children,' she murmured. 'You look as if you have a lot of fun together.'

'We're trying.' Matthew followed her gaze. 'They've not had the best start in life. I'm trying to make it up to them.'

'Oh?'

Josie,' Matthew added urgently, gazing deep into her eyes. 'We need to talk—'

'Matthew, please! I really don't want to. Look, I'm sorry to have interrupted—'

'Will you stop apologising? Can't you see I want you here?' Matthew's dark eyes held her face. 'Stay a while. Please. I really would appreciate it if you would. You heard Josh; he's not exactly enamoured with my ideas for play at the moment.'

'What about...Kathryn?'

Matthew's jaw clenched. 'She's not here. She caught the train to London this morning to visit some friends and see a show. She won't be back until this evening.' He frowned suddenly. 'How do you know her name?'

Josie hesitated, flushing under Matthew's sudden scrutiny. 'She...Kathryn, I mean...visited the agency earlier this morning.'

Matthew raised a dark brow. 'Did she indeed? And what exactly did she have to say?'

'Oh...' Josie lifted her shoulders slightly. 'The usual— you want staff.'

'What sort of *staff*?'

Josie frowned slightly. Matthew didn't seem too pleased. 'Well...a housekeeper, and a nanny, and someone to clean. The usual sort of thing.'

'Have you found anyone yet?'

'No...' Josie hesitated. 'At least, there are a couple of possibilities, but they don't want to live in.'

'*Live in?*' Matthew's voice was steel-edged. He released a taut breath. 'We discussed the possibility of looking for help in the house—a woman who lives locally who could come in and do a bit of cooking, clean and so forth. Certainly nothing on this scale. Forget what Kathryn said.'

'But she was quite insistent.' Josie glanced across at the children and lowered her voice, even though it was doubtful they had heard any of the conversation. 'She was most particular about finding someone to look after the children.'

'Was she?' Matthew looked dauntingly fierce suddenly. He glanced over as Abbie yelled her displeasure at Josh's persistent teasing with the soggy net. 'Find a woman from the village, if you can, but when and if you do, I want you to report to me, not Kathryn. Understood?'

Josie nodded.

He inhaled a deep breath and smiled briefly. 'Thanks. I only have to look at food and I seem to burn it. Charcoal coating covering a delicious raw interior—it's amazing we haven't all come down with food poisoning.' He grinned at Josie's horrified expression. 'No, I'm just kidding. It's not as bad as that—although it's been close on a couple of occasions. The take-away in town is doing a roaring trade because of my bungled efforts in the kitchen.'

'Kathryn doesn't cook, then?' Josie murmured.

There was a pause. 'No.'

'I'm hungry!' Abbie, almost on cue, tugged at Matthew's plaid shirt-tails. 'When's food?'

'It's not that long since breakfast, scallywag!' Matthew scooped Abbie into his arms and looked towards her brother. 'Hungry, Josh?' The boy nodded his head. 'Well, then, do you think, if we all put on our most pitiful expressions, we could persuade Josie to stay for lunch?' Matthew looked across at Josie. 'If she feels really sorry for us, she may even consent to cook.'

'Yeah!' Abbie, hugging Matthew's neck, smiled engagingly. 'Please!'

'What do you say?' His gaze was unflinching, intense. 'See how desperately I resort to underhand tactics? Doesn't that tell you something?'

'Yes.' Josie smiled. 'Yes, it does.'

'Lunch?' Matthew queried. 'You don't have to cook if you don't want to. I can manage a passable omelette if I'm pushed.'

'Lunch,' Josie confirmed. 'And I don't mind cooking.' She inhaled a steadying breath, watching as Matthew swept Abbie onto his shoulders in one effortless movement and took hold of Josh's hand in his. 'Not at all...'

Good going, Mr Fix-it! She's back. You've achieved that much. And she looks a damned sight happier than when she was last inside these walls—but what now?

Matthew watched as Josie, aided by a suddenly helpful Josh, cracked and whisked eggs into a bowl. The house already felt better. And it was probably his imagination, because he wanted her here so much, but the children seemed somehow happier too. The last couple of months had been pretty awful: going over and over that last, badly handled episode, fearful that he would never see her again, that she would never want to see him...

Josie gripped the edge of the work surface and exhaled a long, slow breath. She was mad. *What was she doing here?* Just getting herself in deeper, making everything more difficult, more complicated...

Oh, just to stay here, in the warmth, with Matthew and the children. It was like a pain, this longing, almost too much to bear. Here she was, inside the house she loved most in all the world, with the man that she loved—

She slammed the lid shut on her thoughts. That was the danger—thinking *too* much, dwelling in fantasy land. Hurting herself all over again...

'OK, Josh?' He had looked so troubled earlier. Josie cast a sideways glance at the young boy's face, screwed up with concentration, now, as he whisked the eggs for all he was worth. She sensed definite undercurrents, but had no idea what the problem could be. 'That looks great!' Josie placed an affectionate hand on the boy's shoulder. 'In fact, I don't think I've ever seen such excellent whisking!' She smiled down at the boy's glowing expression. 'Maybe you should take over the cooking. I reckon you could do a pretty good job!'

'Josh's talents know no bounds. You should see some of his drawings; they're excellent.' Matthew retrieved cutlery from a drawer. 'Maybe you could show Josie after lunch,' he suggested.

'You can see our bedroom,' Abbie announced. 'We've got new everything!'

'That sounds exciting.' Josie poured some of the egg mixture into the sizzling frying pan. She surveyed the solid oak units lining one end of the large room, the polished wooden floor scattered with rugs. Her gaze was caught by the flashes of blue and green and yellow in the decor, by the pretty curtains framing the windows, and she knew she couldn't have done a better job with everything even if she had wanted to... It was all so changed from the damp, crumbling mess that Josie had known and loved. If the rest of the house was as good as this... 'After lunch, then, will you show me?'

She was getting in deep. Josie sat on the floor of the children's bedroom and rolled the dice for the umpteenth time.

Matthew's presence opposite was having a debilitating effect—she could hardly concentrate, was often being gently reprimanded by the children for counting the wrong squares, or climbing up a snake when she should have been descending.

Josh won the last of many games, and Josie was glad. She smiled at the boy as they all got to their feet, and then glanced across at Matthew.

'I hope you didn't think I was trying to cheat—I made so many mistakes,' Josie murmured, smiling. 'I haven't played snakes and ladders in years.'

'Neither have I.' There was a slight pause. 'The children have really enjoyed this afternoon.' Dark eyes held her face. 'I appreciate the time you've spent with us.'

'That's OK. I've enjoyed it,' Josie replied softly. 'For a while I could almost kid myself—' She stopped abruptly.

Matthew was silent for a moment, watching her, then he said, 'Kid yourself of what?'

'Oh...' Josie lifted her shoulders in a slight shrug. 'It doesn't matter.' She glanced self-consciously across at the children, who were now delving into a playbox for some toy or other. 'The house is wonderful, by the way,' she added, with determined brightness, conscious that she needed to broaden the conversation. 'Just as I always knew it could be.'

'You always knew?' Matthew's brow creased faintly in query.

'Er...' Josie realised that in her haste she had spoken without thinking. 'Well, after last time...the place is looking really good. You're refurbishing in sections, so I understand?'

'Yes, that's right. Let's sit over here.' Matthew led the way to one of the tall sash windows and gestured to the upholstered seat which had been cleverly designed to make the most of the deep sill. 'Who told you?'

Josie frowned as she sat beside him, conscious of the closeness of Matthew's broad frame, of the way her thigh had no choice but to brush against his. 'Oh...er...one of the girls at work, Susan—the one who gave me the lift that day. Her fiancé is a decorator; he's going to be working on part of the house.'

'I see.'

Josie turned and gazed out of the window. From this bedroom she could see a great deal of the ground surrounding the house. She rested her cheek against the cold pane of glass.

'Penny for them?'

Hearing the soft, deep tones, feeling the vitality of him so close to her, being *here,* at Harcombe Hall—it was almost more than Josie could bear. She shook her head slightly. 'It will be getting dark soon,' she murmured. 'I should be getting back.'

'I'll give you a lift home when Kathryn returns. I was kind of hoping you'd stay until bedtime.' Matthew's voice was quietly seductive.

'Bedtime?' Josie's voice was breathless. 'Matthew, I really don't think—'

He lifted a hand and touched her face, gentle fingers brushing her cheek, sliding down to tilt her chin, so that she had no option but to look into his eyes. 'The children's bedtime,' he added. 'After they're in bed...well, maybe then we'll have a chance to talk.' Dark eyes held her face. 'Now you can't deny that we very much need to do that.'

'I don't see what there is to discuss,' Josie murmured.

'No. I know you don't—that's the problem,' Matthew replied steadily. 'But believe me, we *do* need to talk.'

'What about Kathryn?'

'She's one of the things we need to discuss.'

'No, I meant if she's here—' Josie began.

Matthew's voice was firm. 'Stay.'

She stayed. Selfish need doing battle with her usually prevailing common sense and winning hands down. Matthew's company was like a drug—the more she had, the more she wanted. It made her feel good just being in the same room with him, just seeing him smile, or laugh, hearing the vibrant depth of his voice as he chatted and played with his children.

Josie cooked the evening meal, and they ate all together in the warmth of the kitchen. She pretended they were a family, but she knew, even as she was doing it, that it was a very foolish thing to do...

Chaos ensued after the bedtime routine. Like most pillow fights, it erupted out of nothing and turned into the most enormous fun.

'People will think we're murdering them!' Matthew commented, as one of the children let out an ear-splitting scream of delight and Matthew received yet another direct hit. Josie dodged a blow from Josh, then caught a wild hit on the arm from a giggling Abbie. 'It's years since I had a pillow fight,' she cried, swiping playfully in all directions. 'I'd forgotten how much fun they were!'

'Ah! So you like a bit of good old-fashioned physical violence, do you?' Matthew's expression was teasing. He swung his pillow and caught Josie on the rear.

'Hey!' She retaliated strongly, swinging back for all she was worth.

'You wield a mean weapon, Josie James!' Matthew announced, ducking to avoid a wild blow from Josh. 'That's twice you've caught me!'

'Twice? I've caught you more than that!' Josie, grinning, swung her pillow again, and knocked it with laughing vigour against his broad chest. 'Take that!' she announced playfully. She swung again. 'And that!'

'And that!' Josh joined in, then Abbie, and soon Matthew was under total siege, trying to defend himself from blows at all angles.

'Three onto one—not fair!' he cried playfully. 'I'm going to have to take a hostage!'

He grabbed Josie then, pulling her against his broad chest, removing the pillow from her grasp.

Any excuse to hold her! And to think that after all the meaningless encounters he had imagined himself to be impervious to such strength of feeling, such need...

'Well, it's nice to know I haven't been missed!'

The sound of an unexpected voice, raised above the squeals and shouts, had a sobering effect. Josie, trapped against Matthew's body, could only stand and stare in horror. The children turned and stopped swinging their pillows. Only Matthew seemed unperturbed by Kathryn's impeccably dressed figure standing in the doorway.

'You've missed the fun!' he announced sardonically, making no attempt to release Josie from his grasp. 'Want to join in?'

'I don't think so.' Her voice was icy. 'Not in this suit. Have you seen the mess you've made?' she enquired, glancing at the feathers as they floated down to coat various surfaces. She switched her gaze to Josie and arched a brow. 'Well! Well! The agency girl. Don't tell me this is how you deal with all your clients!'

Josie scanned her brain for a suitable reply, and decided that silence was the most prudent in the circumstances. She pulled against Matthew's hold and he released her.

'Kathryn!' Matthew's voice held a warning note. 'Enjoy the show? Maybe you'd like to get changed out of that very expensive suit, then you can help put the children to bed— read them a bedtime story, perhaps. I said I'd run Josie home.'

'No! No! We don't want Kathryn to read to us; she doesn't do the voices right,' Abbie announced. 'We want you!'

'Abbie!' Matthew shook his head gently.

'Oh, don't worry about it! She's right!' Kathryn's voice was brittle. 'I am useless at reading—in fact I seem to be pretty useless at everything! You were clearly doing very well without me, so I think I'll go. I turned down a dinner invitation as it was to get back here, but now I can see that I may as well accept!'

'Kathryn, for goodness' sake!' Matthew threw her an exasperated glance.

'I don't know when I'll be back!'

'*Kathryn!*' Matthew glowered at the suddenly empty doorway, and then down at Abbie, who was sobbing on the bed. 'Shh! Abbie, there's no need to cry. It's not your fault.'

'Maybe it would be better if I left,' Josie murmured, as she tried to comfort the little girl.

'*Leave?*' Matthew seemed aghast at the idea. He dragged a hand through his dark hair. 'It's dark out now, and I said I'd take you home. Don't leave,' he added quietly, glancing up into Josie's face. 'I'll just go and see if I can talk some sense into Kathryn.'

He was gone a long while. Josie tucked the children into bed and read some of her favourite Winnie the Pooh stories to them. Thankfully they seemed satisfied with her rendition.

She had just dimmed the light to a soft glow, when Matthew entered the room. He looked harassed and tired.

'Josie's reading as good as her pillow fighting, was it?' he whispered as he bent to kiss both sleepy children gently on the forehead. 'They're whacked out,' he commented as he straightened up and turned to face Josie, who was hovering uncertainly nearby. 'I know how they feel.'

'Did you manage to speak to Kathryn?'

'Yes.' Matthew placed a light hand at the small of Josie's back and led her from the room. 'But whatever I said was wrong, and now she's stormed off.'

'Oh! Look, Matthew, I'm sorry if I caused upset. I wish I hadn't stayed now—'

Matthew paused on the landing and turned to face Josie. 'Don't say that. You're not to blame.'

'But it was clear from the way she looked at us that she thought...' Josie's voice trailed to a halt.

'It's not your fault.' Matthew smiled gently. 'Any trouble we have—well, it was there well before you came along.' He lifted a hand to her hair. 'You've got feathers all over you.'

Josie gazed up into his wonderfully handsome face. 'So have you.'

'I've enjoyed this afternoon,' Matthew told her huskily. 'You've no idea how much...' His voice trailed to a halt, dark eyes focused on her mouth. There was a long, long moment of silence. Josie swallowed. Her heart was beating like a hammer in her chest. He was close, not touching, but so close.

'Being with you...' His mouth curved into a vague smile. 'All those years ago—why didn't I notice you then?'

'*Matthew*—'

'Shh!' He pressed a finger to her lips. 'Don't say anything.' He smiled gently. 'I've never been particularly good with words.' Smouldering eyes held hers. 'I kept imagining there would be a right time to explain things properly, but we seem jinxed...' He released a taut breath and shook his head. 'I am so tired,' he murmured. 'So very tired. I've got to go out and find Kathryn.' His gorgeous dark eyes were suddenly bleak. 'You saw what she was like. Believe it or not, beneath that hostile exterior she's a very confused and fragile woman. I've no idea where she could have gone— a bar, maybe, or a hotel. Would you stay with the children whilst I'm gone?'

'Yes. Yes, of course.'

'I'm sorry, Josie. None of this is particularly pleasant, is it? My fault,' he murmured, glancing away. 'I'm handling everything very badly.'

'No—!'

'Yes!' he replied fervently. 'Handling things badly, just like I've always done!'

Josie looked at the clenched jaw, the misery in Matthew's eyes. He was upset about Kathryn, that much was clear. She felt a sudden rush of emotion, and opened her eyes wide to hold back the tears. She ached to be held, to *hold*. An awful wave of self-pity rose up and over-whelmed her. It wasn't fair, she thought miserably. She had so much to give, so much...

'Josie...?'

The way he spoke her name... She closed her eyes, still averting her head, trying so hard not to be affected by the warmth and concern in his voice. It was no good thinking this way. No good at all. Was she mad, risking such weakness with Matthew only feet from her?

'You'd better go,' she whispered croakily. 'You'd better find Kathryn.'

CHAPTER SIX

HE HATED leaving her. God! How he wanted to wrap his arms around her and sink into her softness, and just stay there.

The Range Rover was cold. Matthew turned the heater to maximum and flicked on the headlights.

Where on earth had Kathryn gone? He had his suspicions that there might be someone—a man—although goodness knows who. There had been a couple of phone calls which she'd taken in private, a few unexpected outings recently. She'd certainly lost no time in socialising. What if she had met someone…?

Matthew started up the four-wheel drive and released a breath. He couldn't be sure.

Maybe it was just wishful thinking.

It felt strange being in the house without Matthew. Josie wandered back into the children's room. She felt restless. Her mind kept ranging back and forth over all that had happened. She hardly knew what to think. Matthew liked her, that much was clear—more than liked, he had said…

Josie stopped herself from lingering over his words. The past was the past. The present was what mattered most. And Matthew's present was with Kathryn and the children. It didn't take a genius to see that, despite whatever differences they might seem to have on the surface, Matthew cared about Kathryn. Cared enough to go out into the cold night to look for her.

Josie sat on the window-seat and parted the curtain a little. The moon was a sliver of light in the darkened sky. She looked across at the children sleeping peacefully in their beds and felt the warm trickle of tears rolling down her cheeks.

Josie shook her head. She had no way of knowing what was going on. No one could begin to understand the complexities of another couple's relationship. Guessing wasn't good enough. Hoping...well, hoping made her feel guilty. Matthew and Kathryn lived together as man and wife, with their children.

That was all she had to remember.

Matthew returned some time after midnight. Alone. He had done as much as he could. Kathryn clearly didn't want to be found. He had been everywhere that seemed likely, and a few places that didn't, he'd checked the local hospital, and now all he wanted to do was be under the same roof as Josie and the children.

The house was silent. Matthew moved from room to room, switching off lights, closing doors, looking for her— all the while looking for her.

He found Josie in the children's bedroom, curled up asleep in a large, squashy armchair in the corner of the room, one hand tucked beneath her cheek, silky strands of hair falling sensuously against the slender arch of her throat. Matthew stared down at her sleeping form for a long while, fighting against his desire to wake her, to hold her, conscious that he would be doing so for purely selfish reasons.

He had been so close to kissing her earlier, so close to taking her in his arms. The restraint... Did she know how hard he had had to fight...?

Matthew released a steadying breath. Just thinking about how good it could be between the two of them made the blood rush through his veins.

He left the room, retrieved a couple of blankets from a cupboard on the landing, and draped them gently over her, holding his breath as Josie stirred a little in her sleep. Matthew crouched down beside the chair and watched her for a moment longer, then stood up and silently left the room.

*   *   *

The children were eating a subdued breakfast in the kitchen next morning when Kathryn returned. What conversation there was ceased immediately. Josie, who had been chatting with Josh about the possibility of finding a Christmas tree on the estate, found herself pausing with the butter knife in mid-air.

'Well, isn't this just cosy!' Kathryn threw Matthew a tremulous glance. 'Stay over, did she?'

'Only because I needed someone to look after the children whilst I went searching for you!' Matthew got to his feet. 'Why on earth did you run off like that?'

'Because I could see that I wasn't wanted here, that's why!' Her beautiful face was pinched tight with emotion.

'Kathryn, that's not true...' Matthew's voice was gentle. 'There's no need for you to be like this.'

'Isn't there?' She inhaled a huge gulp of air. 'Well, I think there is!' Her voice quivered noticeably and Josie, despite everything, felt a sudden rush of genuine sympathy for her.

'So where did you get to?' Matthew's eyes were steady on her face.

'I stayed over...with...with a friend.'

'Good friend?' Matthew commented mildly.

'Y-yes. Very!' Kathryn replied sharply. 'I am allowed to *have* friends, presumably?' A quick glance at Josie. 'You seem to be taking full advantage!'

'Kathryn...I was worried about you,' Matthew asserted firmly. 'The children were worried. Please, don't do that again.'

There was a moment of tense silence. Kathryn's face ran the full gamut of emotion as she fought for control. 'I'm sorry Matt,' she murmured quietly. 'I didn't mean...' She stood in the kitchen, dressed smartly in a fine raspberry woollen suit, looking so achingly beautiful and forlorn. Josie swallowed back the lump in her throat. In the agency she had seemed so superior, so in control, whereas now... It wasn't difficult to see, in these moments of vulnerability, how any man could fall for her. 'Sorry for not being....for acting so...so badly,' she murmured brokenly. 'I'm try-ing...trying so hard...' She looked across at him with glis-tening eyes. 'Will you ever forgive me?'

'Kathryn!' Matthew walked towards her then, and held her, stroking her hair, murmuring soothing words of com-fort as Kathryn sobbed into his shoulder.

It was a close, caring embrace that resulted in a turmoil of mixed feelings for Josie. She looked away, and remem-bered the children. She touched them both gently on the shoulder. 'Come on, you two,' she whispered hoarsely, get-ting up from the table and holding out her hands.

'Josh...' Once upstairs, Josie busied herself with straight-ening the children's duvets. 'I'm going to go now. Can you tell Matthew that I'll speak to him another time?'

'Where are you going?' Abbie asked, frowning.

'Home, of course!' Josie forced herself to sound cheerful, even though she felt like throwing herself onto one of the beds and howling like a tormented banshee. 'I've got to go to work this morning.'

'Will we see you again?' Josh asked.

'I hope so.' Josie gave both children a quick hug, con-scious of her unsteady voice. 'Be good!' she added lightly. And without risking another glance at either of them, for fear of embarrassing herself with tears, she ran from the room and skipped lightly down the stairs. She glanced along the corridor which led to the kitchen, thanked heaven that Harcombe Hall was a large house, and left, without being detected, by way of the heavy front door.

'There is a seriously good-looking man in Reception asking for you, Miss James. And when I say good-looking, I mean drop-dead gorgeous!'

'OK, thank you Cathy!' Susan ushered the lively young girl out of Josie's office and closed the door behind her. 'Honestly, that girl!' Susan shook her head. 'I'm surprised you don't have a word with her.'

'She's fine—full of life and always smiling.'

'Which is certainly something that can't be said of you

this morning,' Susan commented dryly. 'What's the matter?
Did you have a bad night?'

'Something like that.' Josie kept her gaze fixed on the
papers in front of her. Her heart was beating wildly, and
her mouth had suddenly gone all dry.

'Seriously good-looking, eh? Only one man I know that
you know fitting that description,' Susan murmured.
'There's Craig, of course, but he's a bit wishy-washy for
my taste.' Susan grinned. 'Shall I send the gorgeous
Matthew in here? Or do you want to go out and greet him
yourself?'

'Actually, Susan…' Josie looked up from her desk and
smoothed a hand across her brow. 'Would you do me the
most enormous favour? He…he doesn't know about me—
I mean about my owning the agency. He thinks I just work
here.'

Susan threw Josie a puzzled look. 'But why on earth
haven't you told him?'

'I don't know.' Josie frowned. 'There was an opportunity
early on—when we first bumped into each other—but I was
angry and stubborn and I let it pass, and now…well…'
Josie shook her head slightly. 'The trouble is, he thinks I
could have done better; I wanted to be a doctor at one
stage—'

'So you're not a doctor, but you've got all this!' Susan
spread her arms wide. 'Honestly, Josie, talk about hiding
your light under a bushel! Fancy not telling him! You are
in one mixed-up state,' she added sternly. 'Has he always
had this effect on you?'

Josie nodded. 'Pretty much. Oh, I know this probably
won't make any sense, but I feel…' Josie paused, trying to
put her thoughts into words. 'It's as if this is my last defence.' Josie's blue eyes were wide; she stared at Susan
earnestly, longing for her to understand.

'*Defence?*' Susan's expression was blank. 'Against
what?'

'When we're together…' Josie's voice was urgent and

low. 'When Matthew…when he looks into my eyes, it's as if…every part of me, all of my emotions are open to him. I feel as if I'm his—absolutely.' Josie managed a pained smile. 'The fact that he doesn't want me, of course is irrelevant. But here…' she glanced around her office '…at work…well, at least in this area of my life I can still create some sort of barrier—a distance—purely because he doesn't know the whole truth.'

'Sort of like a secret weapon?' Susan murmured.

'I suppose so,' Josie murmured doubtfully. 'But even if I did want to tell him the truth, now wouldn't be the right time. I left rather suddenly this morning.' Josie released a tense breath. 'You're right, Matthew does make me a little crazy—turns me upside down so that I can't think straight.' She looked imploringly at Susan. 'So, will you do it for me?'

'Do what?'

'Cover for me?'

'*Cover?* How am I supposed to do that?'

Josie moved from behind her desk. 'Pretend the business is yours.'

'Oh, Josie—!'

'Please!'

There was a knock on the office door at that moment. Josie skipped across the room and began rummaging in one of the filing cabinets, gesturing as she did so to Susan, who, after a brief hesitation, sat in the recently vacated black swivel chair behind the desk.

'Mr Jordan!' Cathy threw Susan a puzzled look, glanced across to Josie and then opened the door wide. 'And entourage!' she announced gaily.

Abbie and Josh entered first, dressed in soft, brightly coloured woollen duffle coats to keep out the cold. Then Matthew, looking as wonderful as ever, dark hair slicked back from his face, wearing a long black leather coat over charcoal-grey jumper and trousers.

'Forgive the interruption.' Matthew looked at Josie for a long moment, then glanced across at Susan and held out his hand. 'We've met, haven't we?' He smiled. 'How are you?'

'Oh, I'm just fine!' Susan shook hands enthusiastically. 'All the better for seeing you,' she added, in her typical blunt manner.

'We're Christmas shopping!' Abbie told Josie with a grin. 'We're going to buy perfume and a necklace,' she added, in whispered tones. 'For you know who!'

'Could we talk?' Matthew's dark gaze returned to Josie's face. 'I tried phoning you at home, but there was no reply. There was no need to rush off like that,' he added quietly.

'I thought there was.' Josie worked hard at showing him a calm expression. In that moment she made her decision. She would be strong, do what she should have done in the first place, as soon as she'd discovered that Matthew...that Matthew had a life, commitments, a relationship—however unstable it appeared to be. 'I've got the details of the house-keeper you wanted,' she added briskly, moving to her desk, rifling through a stack of files. 'I'll give them to you, now you're here. Mrs Milton. She lives in Harcombe village. Would it be OK if I sent her along for a chat this afternoon?'

'Yes.' Matthew inhaled deeply and then nodded. 'But you know I didn't come here for that.'

'You want time on your own!' Susan rose swiftly from behind Josie's desk. 'I'll leave you. Would either of you like a coffee—maybe a drink and a biscuit for the children?'

'None for me, thanks, but the children will probably be happy to have something!' Matthew smiled gratefully at Susan, who blushed with obvious pleasure. 'This very nice lady is offering refreshments,' he informed Josh and Abbie, who were playing with the coloured paperclips on Josie's desk. 'Would you go with her? I won't be long; I just want a chat with Josie.'

'Are you going to come Christmas shopping with us?' Abbie asked as she clambered off a chair.

'No, I can't, I'm afraid,' Josie replied. 'I've got lots of work to do.'

'Have you?' Matthew's gaze was intense once Susan had led the children from the room.

'What?' Josie glanced at Matthew briefly, then sharply away again.

'Got lots of work to do?'

'Yes.'

'Your boss seems like a nice woman,' he murmured. 'Good to work for?'

Josie nodded vaguely. 'Er…yes. Yes, she is.'

'Are you sure she wouldn't give you some time off? If you told her there were extenuating circumstances—'

'But there aren't.' Josie flicked through the filing cabinet and pulled out a file at random.

There was a significant pause. Matthew's voice when he spoke was edged with steel. 'Josie…we have to talk.'

'Aren't we doing that now?' she replied artlessly. 'Look, there's no big deal.' She forced a smile. 'I left this morning because I had work to get to. Kathryn was home. You and she needed time together.' She grabbed another file from the cabinet and began to open it, but the file was suddenly snatched from her hand. She looked up in alarm as Matthew slapped the folders on top of the cabinet and slammed the drawer shut. 'What…what do you think you're doing?' Josie asked shakily.

'Trying to get your attention—what does it look like?' He was angry at last, jaw clenched, dark eyes flashing fire. 'Why are you acting like this? *Why?*' Matthew took a pace towards her, came close, then, clearly thinking better of it, stepped back so that there was more space between them.

Josie swallowed. It took a while for her to think of the right thing to say, and then, when she did speak, she knew, deep down, that she had chosen wrongly. But by then it was too late; the words had been said. 'I don't think it's a good idea that we see each other any more.'

'What?' Matthew looked at her for a long while, mesmeric eyes ranging over her face, studying every inch.

Through the closed door, the clatter of the outside office could be heard.

'I...I don't think—' Josie began

'I heard you.'

'I mean it,' Josie replied quietly, hating the coldness in his voice. 'I...I have my own life to lead.'

'I see.'

No, you don't! Josie cried silently. *Not at all!* She released a taut breath. 'You know, I was glad to meet you again after all those years, but...' Her voice trailed to an awkward halt.

'But you'd prefer it if I kept my distance,' Matthew finished for her in clipped tones.

Josie fought against the selfish desires that were assailing her body and won, but only just. 'Yes,' she replied miserably. 'Yes.'

The phone rang then, a harsh, insistent sound that made Josie jump. She picked up the receiver, listening distractedly to Cathy, who informed her that Craig Taylor was in Reception ready for their meeting at eleven, conscious of the overwhelming presence of Matthew only feet away. As soon as she replaced the receiver he spoke.

'I'm sorry.' His tone was cool, brisk. 'I've assumed more than I had a right to. I'll leave you to get on with your work.'

'Matthew—!'

He turned at the doorway. 'Yes?'

Josie frowned. She didn't know what to say. All she could think of was Kathryn and the children and Matthew, living together at Harcombe Hall. 'Nothing.' She shook her head. 'It doesn't matter.'

His eyes narrowed, piercing her face like shafts of hot steel. He yanked open the door. Beyond, in the outer lobby, stood Craig, the firm's accountant, tall, slim, blond, mildly good-looking—a pale reflection in comparison to Matthew. She saw him cast a swift, distracted glance over Craig, who was chatting easily to Cathy, Susan and the children.

'Time to leave, kids!' His voice was deceptively calm.

Josie watched for a fraction longer as he said a few words of thanks to Susan, and then she turned, conscious of Craig, who was picking up his briefcase and striding towards her office.

'Morning!'

'Hello, Craig.' Josie kept her gaze fixed on the bustling high street outside the window. 'Sorry, I forgot all about you.'

'Story of my life. Who was that?'

'Who?' Josie hoped Craig wouldn't notice the tremor in her voice.

'The chap with the kids who just left.'

'Oh...er...just a client. He's looking for a housekeeper.' Josie inhaled a huge breath and finally turned to face Craig, who was making himself at home by spreading papers over her already filled desk. She might as well tell him now, she thought. Get it over and done with. 'He's the man who's bought Harcombe Hall.'

'Really?' Craig's expression revealed a curious mixture of shock and something that was almost approaching alarm. 'I had no idea.'

'Why should you have?' Josie placed cool fingers to her forehead, oblivious of Craig's frown.

'Nice-looking kids,' he murmured.

'Yes.' Josie's voice was soft. 'Very.'

'Pretty tough, eh?' Craig's tone was sympathetic. 'Having to deal with him. Did you...tell him you wanted to buy the place?'

'No!' Josie shook her head. 'No, I didn't. It's over, done with. I lost it. I don't want anyone to know—especially him!'

'OK! OK! I get the picture.' Craig wandered over from the desk to the window, and looked at Josie at close range. 'I'm sorry, I know the house meant a great deal to you, but—'

'It's not that!' Josie turned from him. 'At least...well, it's part of it...' She fumbled with the catch of the window and opened it, breathing in some of the fume-filled, raw

December air, wishing she were back in the fields around Harcombe Hall. 'But not all.'

'I'm listening.'

Josie shook her head. 'I don't want to talk about it.'

'So, what are you going to do now?'

Josie frowned. 'About what?'

'Well, you've got all that money sitting doing nothing in the bank. Look, I know this might seem a novel idea, especially coming from an accountant, but why don't you spend some of it? Treat yourself to a few little luxuries?'

'I don't know, Craig,' Josie replied wearily. 'I might.'

'Take a look at the car park.' Craig pointed. 'What's that?'

'Your car.'

'And the one next to it?'

Josie shrank back from the window as Matthew and the children descended the steps. 'Another car,' she murmured.

'And what have they both got in common?' Craig asked lightly, oblivious of the tension in Josie's body.

She shook her head. 'I don't know! Look, Craig I'm not in the mood for games.'

'They're both new and shiny and expensive. Now let's cast our eyes over the vehicle *you* insist on driving around in.' Craig, immaculate and, Josie thought, far too obsessed by image, shook his head. 'Honestly, you are one of the wealthiest women I know, and yet you persist with this ridiculously thrifty lifestyle.'

Josie reached forward and yanked the window shut, her eyes glued to Matthew's car as he pulled away from the front of the building. 'I was saving for the house!' she hissed. 'You of all people know that! If you didn't insist on tying up so much of my money in investments—!'

Craig released a patient breath. 'Josie, we've gone over this before. It's sound money-management. Give this business another couple of years and you'll be able to buy a place twice the size of Harcombe Hall.'

I don't *want* a place twice the size of Harcombe Hall. I

want that one!' She held her head in her hands, and immediately felt Craig's comforting arm around her shoulders.

'Sorry! Sorry! I know I can be a bit of a bully sometimes, but I'm just thinking of you, Josie. You drive yourself so hard,' he added gently. 'Isn't it about time you lived a little?'

'Oh, that's rich, coming from a man who gets into his office at seven and rarely leaves before nine or ten o'clock at night!' Josie replied mildly.

'Yes, well, maybe I have overdone it in the past, but recently...well, let's just say I've begun to see the error of my ways. Look,' Craig added brightly, 'I've been invited to a bit of a Christmas bash over at the Cranshaws' on Saturday—you know Nigel and Ruth; he's an investment banker and she runs a clothing business for children from home. You met them at my place in the summer.'

'Yes...yes, I remember,' Josie replied wearily. 'But I honestly don't think I'm in the mood—'

'You will be by Saturday. And besides, what's the alternative—moping around in that ghastly little house of yours?' Craig added bluntly. 'I'll pick you up at eight o'clock. No arguing! See!' He grinned as Josie glanced up into his face. 'I can be totally masterful when I want to!'

She almost didn't go. At seven-thirty Josie was still sitting in front of the television, trying to decide whether she could be bothered or not.

In the end, ashamed because she had never imagined herself to be capable of such an inordinate amount of self-pity, she heaved her unwilling frame from the sofa and headed for the shower.

Craig was on time. Josie heard the beep of his horn as she hastily finished putting the final touches to her make-up.

'Well! Well!' He grinned at her affably from the door-step a moment later. 'Dreadful taste in cars, marvellous taste in clothes. That is a seriously stunning dress! Purple is definitely your colour. I had absolutely no idea.'

'No idea of what?' Josie checked her bag for the key and then closed the front door behind her.

'That you could look so totally glamorous and unbusinesslike! I see the horrible hatchback is still outside,' Craig remarked teasingly as they walked up the front path. 'I had hoped you might have nipped round to the local car dealer after my lecture the other day.'

'I still might!' Josie shivered as the chill of the December evening seeped into her bones, and pulled her matching silk-lined wrap more closely around her body. 'What do you think?' She managed a smile. 'Porsche or Ferrari?'

'Either. Both great for the image!' Craig cast Josie's car a distasteful glance. 'Have you ever thought what impression you give, driving around in that thing?'

'It gets me from A to B. Besides,' Josie replied, 'if you remember, I was saving my money for a reason.'

'Yes, of course.' Craig opened the door of his immaculate BMW for Josie.

'Maybe I will buy a new car,' she announced brightly, conscious that if she didn't make the effort she would sink into the depths of depression again. 'But don't think it's because you persuaded me!' she added lightly. 'I have got a mind of my own!'

Craig sat in beside her. 'Tell me something I don't know!' he murmured dryly as he turned the key in the ignition and the powerful engine roared into life.

I'm in love. Josie stared through the windscreen with misted eyes. *Deeply, frantically, with all of my heart. I'm in love with another woman's man!* she cried silently. *And I don't know what to do about it!*

Nigel and Ruth Cranshaw's home was a stylishly converted old barn, situated on the outskirts of Harcombe village. Josie wondered, as Craig brought the BMW to a halt in the large, walled front courtyard, why she hadn't thought to ask where they lived before now.

'You could have told me.'

'What?' Craig frowned slightly. He stared over the

gleaming roof of the BMW as Josie got out of the car. 'Told you what?'

'That they lived near Harcombe.'

'Sorry.' He lifted his shoulders in a slight shrug, before locking the door. 'I thought you knew. Does it matter, then?'

Josie shook her head, glancing round surreptitiously at the other cars already parked outside the house. 'I just wish you'd mentioned it, that's all. You know how badly I feel about Harcombe Hall, and it's practically just around the corner.'

'A couple of miles at least.' Craig shook his head. 'Honestly, Josie, I'm really surprised at the way you're letting this get to you. There are other houses—and most of them in a damn sight better condition than Harcombe Hall!'

'Will they be here, do you think?'

'Who?'

'Oh, for goodness' sake, Craig, stop being so dense! You know exactly who I mean!' Josie retorted. 'The new owners. Will they be here?'

'Now how am I supposed to know that?' Craig enquired without full conviction. He placed a genial arm around Josie's waist. 'Look, even if they are here, there's no need to look so panicked. I'm certainly not going to mention that you wanted to buy the place, and no one else knows, do they?' Craig's smile was full of good humour. 'Relax! Where's the chew 'em up and spit 'em out attitude that I've come to know and love? Come on!' He hugged her close for a brief moment. 'Let's get inside. I don't know about you, but I could really do with a drink.'

'Lovely to see you again!' Ruth, a slim forty-something, with shiny red hair, welcomed Josie with a warm smile as soon as she crossed the threshold. 'Here, let me take that wrap. Gorgeous dress,' she commented, as Josie slipped it from around her shoulders. 'Something tells me you didn't buy that at the local chain store!'

'No.' Josie smiled distractedly. 'I bought it last year...this is only the second time I've worn it.' Her gaze drifted. The converted barn, high-ceilinged and tastefully decorated, was warm and vibrant with an already large number of well-dressed guests. She hadn't seen either of Matthew's cars outside... She felt ridiculously on edge— just the possibility that he might be here...

'Here! Have a drink. You look as if you need it!' Craig lifted a glass from a passing tray and guided Josie out of the path of more arrivals. 'What's wrong with you? You're in another world; Ruth was talking to you then and you didn't hear a word she was saying!'

'Was she?' Josie glanced back hurriedly. 'I didn't mean to be rude. I...I just had my mind on other things. Did she take offence, do you think?'

'Ruth?' Craig shook his head. 'No, she's not the type. She did give you rather a weird look, though. Honestly, Josie, there I am, always going on about what a brilliant business woman you are, and you act like you're one brick short of a load!'

'Oh, Craig!' Josie frowned. 'Don't be rotten. I don't think I can cope with it tonight!'

'It really is a big thing, isn't it—the fact that you might bump into the recently instated lord of the manor?' Craig eyed Josie's flushed face carefully. 'If I didn't know better, I might be inclined to think that there's a little more to the situation than simple bad feeling about the purchase of a house.'

'Don't be silly!' Josie inhaled deeply. 'Now you're talking rubbish!' She followed Craig over to a space beside the open staircase. 'I thought you understood just how much I wanted that place,' she hissed. 'It...it hurts, that's all...the fact that I'll never be able to live there.'

'Sorry.' Craig leant forward and kissed Josie on the cheek. 'I didn't mean to be a bully. But, honestly, you mustn't be too downhearted; there will be other houses. It's just a case of biding your time and finding the right one.'

'Yes... Yes, I suppose you're right.' Josie forced a smile. 'I'm overreacting, I know that, but—'

She knew. As soon as she saw Craig's face, she knew—

although why he should look quite so mesmerised...
Unless... Yes, of course, any man would be mesmerised at
the sight of her.

Josie glanced towards the entrance, frozen in that moment with her glass of wine halfway to her lips.

Matthew, with Kathryn at his side, was being greeted
enthusiastically by Ruth. Josie felt the weakness of wanting
him flood through her body as her eyes rested on his tall,
dark frame. He looked stunning, dressed in an immaculate
dark suit, with a crisp white shirt and a burgundy silk tie,
dark hair smoothed back casually from his wonderfully
handsome face...

She forgot to breathe. It wasn't fair, she thought, that he
should make her feel this way still—after all these years.
Why couldn't she be immune? Why couldn't she get over
him?

Kathryn, looking as beautiful as ever, dressed in a
pleated sheath of emerald silk, was close by his side, encircled in the protective sweep of his arm. His woman.

Josie glanced at Craig's flushed face. 'Come on!' She
catapulted into action suddenly, taking hold of Craig's arm
and beginning to lead him into the throng of guests in the
main room.

'What are you doing?' He half turned behind her, and
there were two spots of high colour on each of his cheeks.

'I really, really don't want to speak to them!' Josie whispered. 'Oh, Craig!' she wailed quietly. 'How could you do
this to me?'

'Look, believe me, I had no idea he'd be here any more
than you did. Kathryn said—'

'What?' Josie frowned. *'You know her?'*

'No, not really.' He looked vaguely uncomfortable.
'Well...we've met. She was here one day when I was looking over Ruth's accounts.'

Josie glanced over Craig's shoulder and saw that mercifully Matthew and Kathryn had veered off in the opposite
direction. 'Craig, for goodness' sake! Why didn't you mention this before?'

'Because... Well, it didn't seem important.' He released a sigh. 'I had no idea the *two* of them would be here this evening, honestly, Josie!'

'I want to leave.' Josie's voice was hoarse with urgency. She peeped over Craig's shoulder. Matthew, standing tall and strong over the other side of the room, had his back to her, but just casting her eyes upon the line of his broad shoulders sent a tingle of awareness running down Josie's spine.

Kathryn looked beautiful. Josie heaved a steadying breath. It was difficult accepting that the arm curled possessively around Matthew's waist had every right to be there, that however strongly she felt nothing could change the fact that Kathryn was the woman he had chosen to spend his life with. 'Craig...please...would you drive me home? I can say I've got a headache or something, so that Ruth won't be offended—'

'No way!' Craig gritted. 'Why are you letting that man get to you like this?' he enquired, with a tone that bordered on bitterness.

'I've explained—'

'No, you haven't.' He shook his head, his gaze still fixed across the room. 'Look, I don't want to pass judgement, but I think you're taking this to the extreme.' He glanced briefly down into Josie's face, took a healthy mouthful of red wine. 'So the man has it all! Beautiful house, wonderful woman, gorgeous children. Well, I'm not leaving on his account,' he added, with uncharacteristic fire, 'and neither, if you've got any sense, will you!'

CHAPTER SEVEN

'CRAIG, it's not that simple!'

'Why isn't it?'

Josie heaved a breath. There was no way she could reveal her innermost thoughts to Craig—she hardly dared reveal them to herself. 'Can't you just accept,' she murmured, 'that I don't want to talk to him, for whatever reason?'

'Too late, I'm afraid,' Craig informed her, under cover of taking a drink. 'He's seen you and he's coming over. Actually,' he added, with a definite lack of his usually smooth assurance, 'I think it's best if I leave you both to it. I could really do with another glass of wine…'

'But… *Craig?*' Josie frowned in dismay as he melted from her side. What was wrong with him all of a sudden?

She didn't know what to do. Josie wanted to turn around, but she could barely move. She stood rigidly, wine glass gripped in one hand, every nerve-end alert for the sound of his voice, the overwhelming force of his presence…

'Hello, Josie.'

She didn't reply for a long moment, using the precious seconds to haul the breath back into her body, to assume the stance of a woman in control. Slowly she turned, aching, constantly aching. Hoping that Matthew wouldn't be able to look into her eyes and understand every thought.

'Hello.'

He looked at her without haste, dark eyes drinking in every aspect of her face and figure. 'You look…' his voice was low, rich, unhurried '…different.'

'Do I?' Her voice sounded shy and breathless. It could have been ten years before, she felt so gauche and susceptible standing before him.

'Nice dress.' His eyes scanned the sumptuous fabric, the

111

elegance of the cut, returned to rest on her face. 'You look…amazing,' he added softly.

'*Oh!*' Josie could hardly breathe. It was as if…as if they were the only two people in the room. The strength of his gaze… She wanted to move towards him, press herself against the strength of his body, touch his face with her hands. He was looking at her… *Oh, goodness!* He shouldn't look at her like that… She could read every thought…

Josie inhaled sharply. She had to be strong. She had to remember the futility of allowing her desires to take a hold. 'Oh, well,' she replied, with a breathless kind of gaiety which fooled neither of them, 'it's surprising what a posh frock can do for a girl.'

'Indeed…' Matthew's eyes lingered once more on the rich velvet, the quality of the line and fabric. 'I only wish it had been for my benefit.' He smiled, and there was a hint of regret in the sensuous eyes. 'You're with someone.'

She was. Of course. Why should he have been surprised to see her talking intimately with another man? He had spotted her almost immediately. It was as if a light shone all around her, illuminating the area in which she stood. He had played it cool—or at least tried to. Acting normally, smiling when spoken to, refusing to give in to his impulse to rush across the room and take her in his arms.

She had hurt his pride the last time they had met—no, it was more than just hurt pride; he had been devastated that she didn't want to see him again, had retreated through shock and hurt, but mostly because of the pain in her expression. He had done that to her, entangled Josie in the mess that was his life. There was no reason in the world why he should expect her to put up with the complications of his situation. No reason at all…

He had imagined…well, perhaps he had imagined exactly what suited him—wanting something so badly it hurt didn't always mean you deserved to get it.

'He's a lucky man.'
  'Who is?'

'Your partner—the guy who seemed rather keen to avoid me. Didn't I see him at the agency?'

'Craig?' Josie glanced across the room, as if looking for him, although in truth she was simply trying to alleviate the pressing need she felt to throw herself into Matthew's arms. 'Oh, he's just my…just a friend,' Josie corrected hastily. She took a mouthful of wine and continued to avoid Matthew's gaze, because looking into his eyes was proving to be too torturous.

'You'd rather we hadn't met here tonight?'

'Oh…no. I…' She didn't know what to say—whether to speak the truth—the real truth. That she longed for him, yearned for him, that a minute didn't go by without him being in her thoughts. Tell him that? Have to live with the consequences?

'No idea what to say?' His smile was gentle, but there was a glint of steel in his eyes. 'You don't look particularly happy. Would you prefer it if I just walked away and left you in peace?'

'No!' Josie, aware of her fervent reply, blushed and shook her head. 'No,' she murmured quietly. 'Please…!' She hesitated, unsure of what it was she wanted to say. Matthew was looking at her, and his gaze was dark and deep, and more than a little dangerous. 'It's just…'

'Just what?'

'I…I didn't expect to see you here, that's all,' she replied miserably.

'Like I said.' Matthew's tone was dry. 'You don't look particularly happy.'

An awkward silence fell between them. Josie felt the panic rising within. If he left her now, somehow she knew that would be it—they would probably have nothing more to do with each other ever again. 'Who's looking after Josh and Abbie?'

Matthew looked at her blankly for a moment, then inhaled a deep breath, as if summoning the resources to answer such an obviously contrived question. 'The miraculous Mrs Milton.' He smiled, but it was clearly strained. 'Thanks for hunting her out, she's been brilliant. The children love her.'

'I'm glad.' Josie smiled as best she could. 'So…so everything's running smoothly now, is it?'

Smouldering dark eyes bit into her. 'Oh…like clockwork,' he replied dryly. 'We're just one big happy household.'

'Matthew…' Josie hesitated, disturbed by the sarcasm in his voice. 'I'm sorry—about the way I was in the office. I didn't mean…' She heaved a breath. 'I didn't mean to be so…so abrupt.'

'But you meant what you said?'

Josie inhaled a deep breath. She had to be strong. She had to stop this thing before it got too far. 'I—'

'Hello! How are you both?' Josie looked up in dazed surprise as their hostess descended upon them. She had been so wrapped up in Matthew and their conversation she had almost forgotten where they were. Ruth Cranshaw beamed, first at Josie and then at Matthew. 'I didn't realise you two knew one another,' she announced, in her rather too loud voice. 'Well!' She slipped an arm around Josie's shoulders and fixed Matthew with her no-nonsense gaze. 'What do you think of our wonderwoman, then?'

Matthew frowned slightly over the rim of his glass. 'I beg your pardon?'

'Josie!' Ruth Cranshaw's voice held disapproval. 'Don't tell me she hasn't told you! But I thought you had Marge Milton from the agency working for you?'

'Yes, I do.' Matthew's voice was polite, although Josie, after a hurried glance, could see the growing puzzlement in his eyes.

'Good worker, that woman. She used to clean and cook for me until Nigel insisted we tighten the pursestrings.' Ruth Cranshaw beamed again, revealing horsey teeth. 'This gorgeous, talented creature! I only wish I had her business acumen. How many branches is it you have now?' she asked brightly.

'Er...' Josie tried to swallow, but suddenly her throat was very tight. She avoided Matthew's gaze. 'Three,' she murmured after a moment.

'And another at Overton soon, so Craig tells me! Voted Young Business Woman of the Year in one of the glossy magazines earlier this year,' Ruth informed Matthew cheerfully. 'Such a good role model for all the young women in the area—not to mention the men, of course!' she added brightly, clearly oblivious of the tension she had caused. 'And so modest with it!' She beamed up at him, clearly waiting for a comment which never came. 'Well, I'll leave you two to carry on with whatever it was you were talking about, if I may,' she continued, somewhat awkwardly. 'Lots of guests—must keep circulating!' She began to move away, frowning slightly at both Matthew and Josie. 'Enjoy the evening...!'

'*Matthew!*' Josie's voice held a strong note of pleading. 'Please! Don't look at me like that. I was going to tell you, but—'

'But what?' He came closer, loomed above her, holding her with the strength of his gaze, the magnetism of his presence. 'You forgot? Tut! Tut! And you such a marvellous business woman and role model!' He was being a little cruel, but somehow he didn't seem able to stop himself. What was that saying? Matthew thought. You always hurt the ones you love...?

'This dress...' He ran a finger over the strap at her shoulder, brushing the smoothness of her skin so that Josie shivered beneath the provoking lightness of his touch. 'Such a contrast to the way you were when I first met you. Tonight you looked so...' A slight curl of his lips. 'Well, it was as if you were someone else—now, of course, it all makes sense.' His voice hardened noticeably. 'You *are* someone else.'

'What do you want?' Josie enquired tautly. 'Do you expect me to apologise—is that it?' she demanded, almost wildly. 'Because, frankly, I don't see why I should have to give you any explanation. You assumed certain things, practically told me I wasn't capable of achieving anything simply because I failed my exams when I was sixteen, and I chose not to enlighten you. That's all!'

'You lied to me,' Matthew's voice was even—too even, maybe. 'You of all people. I thought our relationship was better than that.'

"Our relationship'?' He could say something as cruel as that to her? Josie shook her head. 'It's not my fault you jumped to conclusions!' she repeated angrily.

'No.' Matthew drained his glass. 'You're right. It's not.'

'You'd prefer it that I *wasn't* a success?' Josie queried. She could feel her blood rising. It wasn't fair that he should look at her this way, as if…as if she had committed some crime, or something. 'You'd find it easier if I was still the simple little schoolgirl you left behind?'

'I'd find it easier if you'd told me the truth, that's all!' Matthew replied curtly.

Josie felt the tears filling her eyes. She didn't know what to say, how to explain so that everything would be all right—so that Matthew would stop looking at her with that cold expression in his eyes.

The sound of glass ringing above the hum of conversation was a sudden distraction. Josie glanced across the room. Ruth was in organisational mode once again. 'Food is now being served!' she announced. 'Do please come and help yourselves!'

'Excuse me!' Josie cast agonised eyes at Matthew, and then looked quickly away again. 'I think I'll… Excuse me!' she repeated, and fled, quickly, diving in amongst the other guests as they began to move forward towards the dining area.

She felt miserable. Utterly, utterly miserable. Nothing she seemed to do, or say… Josie dragged a hand through her hair. It was so unfair. She had been so strong recently, and now this. Nothing was ever going to go right between them. She might as well accept that now. All her dreams about seeing him again had turned into a nightmare. Even something which should have been reasonably pleasurable, such as telling Matthew what a success she had made of her life, had been spoilt by her own stupidity.

She inhaled a ragged breath. It was hot in the house, and she felt suddenly nauseous. She needed fresh air. She threaded her way through the groups of people and headed for the front door.

Outside, rectangles of light from the house flooded the courtyard, but Josie headed for the shadows...

'Josie!' Matthew listened to his own voice echoing around the courtyard. Was she out here? Would she be able to detect the urgency in his voice—the despair he felt at having ruined everything again?

He had been taken aback by the revelation. It had wrong-footed him, made him act badly. He couldn't deny that it had been a shock. All that talk about not knowing her—it was fear, he knew that. She was a business woman—a rich one, presumably—and that carried a lot of baggage. In the woods on that first morning...he had been totally attracted by her simplicity, her sweet, girlish charm. It had been like stepping back in time—a chance to rectify the fact that he hadn't noticed her all those years ago. To find out so abruptly, and from someone else, that she was not what he had imagined her to be...

He called her name again, pacing between the cars. Why couldn't she have told him herself? He hated the fact that there were secrets between them—that was why the situation between Kathryn and himself had to be resolved.

Matthew called her name once more. He couldn't go on like this. He needed Josie. He needed her so much...

She watched him retrace his steps and go back into the house. It had taken a mountain of will-power not to step out into the light. She had wanted to, but there were other people to consider, other needs besides her own selfish ones. She couldn't be a home-wrecker. She couldn't bring devastation into the lives of those sweet, innocent children—for they would be devastated, she knew that—had known it all those years ago, when her father had walked into the kitchen one sunny afternoon and told her mother he had found someone else. She remembered the desolation, the fear of losing them both. How could she do that to Josh and Abbie? How?

'Have you seen Josie?'

Craig closed the door of the bedroom behind him. 'Not recently, no. Why? What do you want with her?'

'Did she come here this evening in her own car?'

'No, with me. Look…' Craig stayed firmly in front of the door, his voice wavering slightly. 'Josie doesn't want to have anything to do with you; she's told me that much—'

Matthew's voice was steely. 'Has she indeed?'

'Yes.'

'Did she have a wrap, or was she wearing a jacket with that dress?'

'Er…a wrap.' Craig frowned up at Matthew. 'Why?'

'Get out of my way.'

'What are you doing?' Craig's voice rose in alarm as Matthew made as if to go past him.

'Josie's wrap—I want it.' Matthew's gaze was steely. 'Any objections?'

'No—no, of course not. I'll…I'll get it for you.'

'Here.' Craig reappeared a few moments later and handed the item to Matthew.

'Thanks.' He took it from him. 'You found that very quickly.' His mouth twisted into a deadly smile. 'If I had a suspicious mind, I'd almost imagine you'd had help.'

Colour suffused Craig's normally pale face. 'I don't know what you're talking about—!'

'Just be sure you know what you're doing.' Matthew took a pace towards him, speaking quietly, but not without a hint of a threat. 'And make sure you treat her well, or you'll have me to answer to.'

She was freezing. What had been the point in coming outside? She should have just gone straight to the telephone and called a taxi. And that was exactly what she was going to have to do right now.

Josie stepped into the hallway. Her fingers were stiff and awkward. She picked up the receiver and began to dial, only to find the connection cut after a moment. She stared down at the large tanned hand covering the telephone.

'I've been looking for you.'

'I know.' Her voice was small and miserable.

'You look cold.'

'I am.'

'Home.' Josie held her breath as Matthew draped the wrap around her chilled shoulders. His voice was firm. 'Now. With me.'

Josie frowned. 'But…but what about Kathryn?'

'Kathryn?' He seemed clearly to have forgotten all about her. 'She's…otherwise engaged.'

'What does that mean?' Josie pursed her lips.

'It means Kathryn wants to stay at the party and I don't,' Matthew replied curtly. Josie glanced up into his face and trembled at the sight of such obviously restrained anger. 'It means…' He released a breath of pure tension. 'It means we have time to talk.'

'Matthew, I can't accept a lift home,' Josie told him firmly. 'It…it wouldn't be right.'

'*Right?*' He shook his head in perplexed amazement. 'What are you talking about?'

'You know!' Josie's voice was agonised. 'I can't cope with this.'

'Josie, sweetheart!' Matthew took hold of her arms and turned her round to face him. 'We need to talk.' His mouth curved into a smile that was part humour, part agony. 'I know I've been saying this ever since we met, but if we don't straighten a few things out—'

'Don't call me sweetheart!' Josie replied in frustrated anger, all too aware of the scorch of his hands on her skin. 'I can't go home with you and that's all there is to it!'

Matthew's mouth tightened. 'You know, Josie, I had no idea you could be so stubborn!'

'Well, too bad!' Josie inhaled a ragged breath. She glanced into his face and found this level of torture could make her cruel. 'You have no idea about a lot of things!'

'Which is why we are going to talk! Now, believe me, I can be just as stubborn—more so, probably, than you,' Matthew gritted. 'So I suggest that unless you want a small, but entertaining scene—and a business woman of your un-doubted stature would never want that,' he added sardoni-cally, 'you do the sensible thing and allow me to drive you home!'

'I've told you!' Josie, as always where Matthew was con-cerned, was finding anger to be a strong ally. 'I'm going to call a—!'

'OK, if that's the way you want it!' With one deft move-ment, Matthew bent forward and scooped an astonished Josie into his arms.

'What do you think you're doing?' she cried. 'Put me down this instant!'

'When we get to the car,' Matthew replied evenly. 'Not until then.'

Josie considered struggling, but the firm hold Matthew had on her wasn't going to allow much leeway 'Put me down at once!' she repeated. 'You're being outrageous!'

His mouth curved into a disarmingly attractive smile. 'You think so?' He shook his head, dark eyes sparkling mischievously. 'You ain't seen nothing yet!'

'How could you do that to me?' Josie's indignation came out as a high-pitched squeak as they crossed the courtyard. 'Everyone saw!'

'Who cares? It will give them something to talk about for the rest of the evening.'

'I have got a reputation to consider,' Josie retaliated, somewhat pompously. 'And so have you,' she added sharply. 'Or have you conveniently forgotten that? What on earth are people going to *think*?'

'I don't give a damn what they think!' Matthew stared down into Josie's face. 'And I don't believe you do either.'

'I have to work in this community!'

'Oh, yes. How could I forget that?' Matthew's tone was dry.

'You're not being fair!' Josie pressed a hand against her mouth. She couldn't cope with this any longer. She was going to cry.

'Life isn't fair!' Matthew halted as they reached his Jaguar. 'Look at me, Josie,' he commanded. She did so, blue eyes misted with tears. 'Don't fight it any longer,' he whispered, 'it's too hard. You and I...' His voice trailed to a halt. He placed Josie on her feet, encircling her waist. 'Everything will be all right,' he murmured gently, looking deep into her eyes. 'I promise.' He lowered his head and kissed her gently on the lips. 'You're just going to have to trust me. Can you do that?'

CHAPTER EIGHT

'HOME, then,' Matthew murmured gently as he got in the car. 'You look tired,' he added, glancing across at Josie in the seat beside him. 'Busy week? Lots of high-powered meetings and executive decisions?' The teasing note in his voice was unmistakable. He manoeuvred the Jaguar smoothly out of its parking space. 'I haven't said,' he murmured, 'and you might have thought otherwise, but I'm very impressed with all that you've achieved. *Josie?*' She had been looking out of the window, unsure of her ability to keep her emotions in check, extremely conscious of his arm draped casually along the back of her seat. She turned and glanced into his face. 'You're amazing,' he told her softly. 'Do you know that?'

'Lucky,' Josie replied quietly, 'that's all.' She lifted her shoulders in a small shrug. 'Right place, right time—anybody could have done it.'

'But not just anybody did.' Matthew surveyed her in silence for a long moment, then thrust the car into first gear and pulled away from the courtyard.

They didn't converse on the journey home, which was just as well because Josie needed time—time to sort out the maelstrom of mixed emotions which were hurtling around her body. She wanted him so much it hurt. She loved him with every fibre of her being. But she was frightened—of rejection, of not being all that he wanted, of risking emotions which had been held in check for so long. Of hurting others.

As the Jaguar pulled up outside Josie's home she turned in the half-darkness, propelled by her desire to do the right thing—whatever that was, she thought miserably. 'Thanks for the lift.'

'*"Thanks for the lift"?*' Matthew's tone held amusement. 'Do I detect a note of farewell in that statement?'

'It is getting late,' Josie murmured. 'Maybe you should…'

He waited patiently, half turning towards Josie. 'Maybe I should—what?' he murmured eventually, when it became clear she wasn't going to finish.

Josie inhaled a small breath. 'Go,' she whispered.

'Is that what you *really* want? No, don't answer that,' Matthew corrected, with a smile, 'because whatever you say I'm coming inside.'

Josie's mouth curved slightly. 'Now you're trying to be masterful.'

'*Trying?*' His dark eyes sparkled humorously, sending a stab of awareness through Josie's body. He opened the car door and got out, prompting Josie to do the same.

'So why live here?' he enquired as he accompanied her down the front path.

'Why not?' Josie paused at the front step and rummaged in her small velvet bag for the house key 'It's a roof over my head.' She thrust the key in the lock and pushed open the door, conscious of Matthew following close behind. She was weak, she knew that, but, oh, it was difficult—*so* difficult! All she wanted to do was throw herself into his arms. Did he know that? Could he feel the heat rising from her body in the confines of the narrow hallway?

Still, she made the effort, worked hard at appearing cool and in control, even when she heard the click of the front door and knew they were finally alone together. 'I suppose now you're going to enquire why I don't live somewhere a little more befitting my status, or some such rubbish,' she added waspishly.

'Hey! It was an innocent question.' Matthew stood for a moment and surveyed Josie with a smile. 'Don't start reading more into it than I meant. Or I may begin to get the impression that you're looking for areas of conflict just so that you'll have an excuse to throw me out!'

Josie flicked on a light at the end of the hallway, and

turned after a moment to face Matthew with arched brows. 'Who said I need an excuse?'

If only he wouldn't smile at her like that—so...so mischievously. It took her back to the old days: glimpses of him astride his motorbike, helmet under one arm, laughing with his mates on one or another street corner. Or, as on one memorable occasion, emerging unexpectedly from a shop on the high street with his arm draped casually around a girl.

Josie remembered the thrill of the moment. She had blushed, spent precious seconds agonising over whether to say hello, decided there was little point because he wouldn't recognise her, and if he did she'd die because she looked an absolute fright, by which time Matthew had stopped— *actually stopped*—smiled and asked how she was doing. She'd mumbled some inadequate reply—a source of extreme annoyance for days after—where had her wit and intelligence been when she'd needed them most?—and watched, standing in the middle of the pavement in stupefied pleasure, as Matthew and the girl walked on, her heart thudding, her body pulsing with hormones and delight. And then, just when she'd thought the thrilling encounter had come to an end, Matthew had glanced over his shoulder and winked at her. Dangerous.

'Penny for them?'

'Too precious for a penny,' Josie murmured. 'I was thinking about my youth,' she added, pushing the door open and moving through into the sitting room. 'Juvenile stuff, most of it: daydreams and fantasies. I seemed to spend most of my time living in another world.'

'Was the real one so bad, then?' Matthew, standing tall and strong, seemed to dwarf the size of Josie's compact living space.

'Oh...you know,' she replied evasively. 'The usual sort of thing.'

'Actually, I don't.' Dark eyes held her face. 'In some ways I feel as if I've known you all my life, and in others I feel as if I hardly know you at all.'

'You're referring to the agency,' Josie murmured. 'Look, I know I acted foolishly, but—'

'I'm not talking about that.' Matthew's voice was mild. He took a pace towards Josie, who was standing awkwardly in the middle of the room. 'It's about more than that,' he repeated, 'you know it is.'

'I'll make us a drink!' Josie released a ragged breath, thought about fleeing through the archway which linked the sitting room with the kitchen, but found her whole being rooted to the spot as Matthew came close.

'I want to know you,' he told her huskily. 'All of you. Every breath, every heartbeat...' He didn't touch her, but his voice was like a caress, so hypnotic, so seductive. Josie wanted to melt right there and then. If he reached out and touched her, she would be lost. Right or wrong—she knew she would not be able to resist.

'You look unhappy.' He frowned, dark eyes resting intently on her face. 'I've made you look that way. When I first saw you, in the wood you looked so animated, radiating contentment and joy.'

'I'm just tired. I... I...' Josie shook her head, lost for words. She couldn't think when Matthew looked at her in such a way. 'Don't,' she whispered, placing two hands over her eyes. 'Please don't!'

'Don't what?' He touched her then. Strong hands peeled away the shield she had erected from her face. 'You think it's that easy—that I haven't tried?' His voice was gruff with intensity. 'Josie, we've got to deal with the things that life throws up at us the best way we can—you and I both know that. The bad, the good...' Strong fingers interlaced with hers, Matthew manoeuvred Josie back against the wall near to the arch, and, raising her hands, held them prisoner above her head. 'Like now,' he said huskily, brushing his mouth against her lips.

'I want it to be good,' Josie asserted shakily. 'You don't know how much. But—' She finally found the strength to avoid his mouth, turned her head to one side, a tortured expression on her face. 'I can't, Matthew! Don't you understand? I'm not that…not that sort of girl!' she finished harshly. 'I've lived my whole life with a father who thought nothing of the commitments he had made to my mother!' Josie heaved a ragged breath. 'You and Kathryn have made a commitment to one another; you have children, you live together, and we just…we just can't do this!'

He silenced her then. Taking swift and uncompromising possession of her mouth, kissing her with lethal sensuality, so that Josie thought of nothing except that moment, the feeling of sexy roughness and desire as Matthew pressed his muscular frame against her yielding body.

'This is just the beginning,' he whispered, his lips less than a kiss away. 'I promise you that…'

'Matthew…' Josie, wide-eyed and breathless, inhaled a ragged breath. She felt drunk, dazed, hardly able to think coherently. 'We shouldn't be—'

'We should…' His mouth covered hers, briefly at first, and then again, touching, tasting, exploring every contour… 'I'm a good guy, Josie. Can't you trust me?'

'Matthew…please!' His name came out sounding taut and strained. 'I really don't think…' she gasped a breath as his mouth took possession once again '…that this is a good idea!'

'You will.' He drew his head back and looked at her, and his smile was soft and sensuous. 'You will when I've explained.'

'What?' she whispered, almost miserably. 'What is there to explain?'

Josie watched with a mixture of apprehension and excitement as Matthew kissed her mouth again, then lifted a hand and brushed a strand of hair from her face.

'Everything,' he murmured. 'Absolutely everything.'

He felt happy. Just anticipating what he was about to tell her made him feel good. As if a weight was about to be lifted from his shoulders. He needed her. *So much*. He couldn't endure another moment without her. She looked so lost, so confused. He wanted to make everything right.

He wanted her. Now. This moment. But he had to be patient. He had to explain...

Smouldering eyes held Josie's face for a long moment, and then Matthew spoke, softly, seriously, clearly. 'Kathryn is not Josh and Abbie's mother. She and I are not lovers.' He paused, time enough to allow the words he spoke to sink in. 'There is no romantic involvement between us.'

Silence. Josie looked at him in growing astonishment. 'But I...I thought...' She shook her head slightly. 'But she said—'

'Kathryn?' Matthew frowned. 'What did she say?'

'When she came to the agency that day, to ask about a housekeeper and nanny...' Josie's voice was small. 'There was a ring on her finger and she made it clear that you and she were...I thought you were married. That Josh and Abbie were your children.'

'Not even close.'

Josie inhaled a breath. 'It's not true?' she whispered. 'Not any of it?'

'No.' Matthew dropped a kiss onto her mouth. 'Not any of it. Kathryn is the children's aunt. Her sister was their mother. Come on...' He pulled her towards the lounge. 'It's a complicated situation. We'd better sit down.'

'But I don't understand.' Josie walked in a daze and sat beside Matthew on the sofa. 'Why would Kathryn...? I don't understand,' she repeated, turning to look into the handsome face.

Matthew ran a hand over his face. 'Abbie and Josh...' He shook his head slightly. 'Their parents were killed in a road accident just over a year ago.'

'*Their* parents?' Josie stared at Matthew in amazement 'You're not...you're not their father?' she whispered. 'But Abbie calls you Daddy?'

Matthew's eyes lingered intently on Josie's face. 'I know she's started to do that lately. But I'm their guardian. Angus—their real father—was my friend as well as my business partner.'

'And Kathryn's their guardian too?' Things were beginning to fall into place—or so Josie thought.

'No. That's where the complication begins,' Matthew replied. 'Angus and I had a conversation many months before he and Julia—his wife—were killed. His mother had not long died, and he had been getting his personal affairs in order—updating his will, that sort of thing. He asked me then how I would feel about becoming the children's guardian, should anything happen to him or Julia. I thought about it for a couple of days, and said yes.' Matthew's gaze was bleak. 'They were both in their thirties; you don't seriously imagine something like this is ever going to happen...' His broad chest rose as he inhaled a deep breath. He loosened his tie and leant back against the sofa. 'But it did,' he murmured, half to himself. 'It damn well did...'

'Those poor children,' Josie murmured. She was still struggling to come to terms with the bombshell that Josh and Abbie had suffered such a loss. 'They must have been in torment.'

'Yes.'

The room was very quiet. In the silence, Josie tried to imagine how awful it must have been for Josh and Abbie, and knew she couldn't come anywhere close.

'There were so many dark days after their parents were killed,' Matthew continued in quiet tones. 'Kathryn and I did the best we could, but it was difficult. We struggled along as a sort of makeshift family for the first year or so, then one day I decided to return home.'

'With the children *and* Kathryn?'

Matthew looked at Josie. 'Yes.'

'They needed her—or at least that's what I thought—as much as they needed me. And Kathryn was grieving too. She had lost her only sister.' He ran a hand through his dark hair, a gesture from the old days that had always, *would* always turn Josie's insides to mush. 'In hindsight I can see that neither of us were thinking straight. I was just trying to do what was best for the children. Although they lived almost all of their lives in South America, they were born here and they visited frequently. So I thought a fresh start, an adventure. Something different to focus on.'

'Their mother—Julia—she was South American, though?' Josie asked.

'Partly.' Matthew nodded his head. 'She was born in England. Her father was Brazilian and her mother English. Angus was English.'

'I'm still…' Josie glanced at Matthew '…confused. Why did Kathryn say that you and she were…together?'

Matthew heaved a breath. 'I don't know. We saw each other a couple of times, but it was a lifetime ago—long before this tragedy happened—and it wasn't serious. At least not on my part. I made it clear from the outset that the only reason I agreed to Kathryn living with us was for the children. She hadn't had much to do with them when they were younger, but she was—*is*,' Matthew corrected, 'their aunt. And I thought that counted for something—I thought at the very least it would be what Julia would have wanted.'

'Why didn't they make Kathryn the children's guardian?' It was an obvious question, and one which Josie knew she should have thought of before.

'I don't know—or at least I didn't think I did.' Matthew shook his head. 'But the time we've spent together… Now things are a little clearer. Maybe because she's as she is: flighty, self-obsessed—'

'Not just *self*-obsessed,' Josie murmured.

'No.' Matthew's voice was flat. 'But she can be fun too—used to be. And she can be kind and thoughtful.' He shook his head. 'The tragedy really affected her badly.'

'So, for the past year you've been struggling to deal with all this.' Josie looked into Matthew's handsome face and spoke softly. 'When we first met…I thought you looked tense.'

'*Tense?*' His mouth curved—half-smile, half-grimace. 'I was an emotional wreck! Still am, but I'm getting there,' he murmured. 'My recovery has something to do with a beautiful young tycoon who has the bluest eyes I think I've ever seen.'

'I wish I could make it all better,' Josie whispered softly.

'You can't—no one can. But what you can do is stop feeling guilty over our involvement.'

'Are we involved?' Josie looked into his stunning eyes, and knew that she couldn't be more involved if she tried.

'What do you think?' Matthew murmured as he pulled her to him. He kissed her with a slow, lingering sexuality, lean, strong hands moving with subtle purpose over Josie's heated skin.

She was drowning, falling against him, *into* him. This was what she had been waiting for—for all of her life. This moment, free to want him, to love him, falling...falling...

And then the phone rang.

Josie tensed as the harsh, persistent ring shattered the perfection of the moment. She tried to ignore it—they both did—but finally Matthew lifted his mouth from hers. 'You'd better answer it.'

'The answer-machine will cut in after the tenth ring,' Josie whispered.

'Even so...' Matthew glanced at his watch and cursed softly beneath his breath. 'It's later than I thought.'

'The children...you have to get back.' Josie stretched across the sofa and lifted the receiver. She couldn't feel jealous or annoyed about that. In fact, after the wonderful news that Kathryn and Matthew weren't even remotely involved, she doubted whether she'd ever feel miserable again. 'Hello?'

'Is he there?'

It wasn't Mrs Milton, as Josie had half expected, but Kathryn herself, sounding belligerent and more than a little drunk.

Josie's heart thudded, but she managed to keep her voice calm. 'Yes, I'll just get him for you.'

'Before you do,' Kathryn added in acid tones, 'maybe you and I should have a little talk.'

'I don't think we've got anything to say—'

'Just remember,' Kathryn continued, 'you're not the first and you certainly won't be the last. He'll fool you just like he did me, with talk of needing and wanting, but you'll get discarded, just like I was, and then where will you be?'

Josie removed the receiver from her ear and held it towards a concerned-looking Matthew. 'It's Kathryn,' she informed him in neutral tones. 'She wants to speak to you.'

Matthew took the phone from her, glancing at her with a slight frown. 'Are you OK?'

'Yes!' Josie smiled. 'Of course. I'll just go into the kitchen.'

He caught her hand as she walked by, tugged her to him and kissed her mouth with the sort of passionate warmth which needed no words to accompany it.

In the kitchen, Josie filled the kettle for lack of anything else to do. She didn't want to listen to their conversation, or dwell on Kathryn's bitter words. She didn't want anything to spoil the way she was feeling right now.

After a brief moment she felt the much needed strength and warmth of Matthew's arms around her waist. He pressed his mouth against her golden hair. 'I've got to go.'

'Yes.' Josie leant her head back against his broad chest and closed her eyes, revelling in the feeling of his presence, trying hard not to think about the way Kathryn had sounded, what she had said. 'The children need you.'

'I don't want to leave you.' He pushed back her hair and kissed her neck, the bare skin of her shoulder, tracing invisible patterns with his mouth so that Josie's body trembled with need and desire. 'Do you know how badly I want to make love to you?' he asked huskily.

Josie smiled. 'I think I've got some idea,' she murmured.

'Will you come over to the house tomorrow? In the morning—early. It's Sunday. We can spend the whole day together.'

'You, me, Josh, Abbie *and* Kathryn?'

'I will sort it out.' Matthew turned Josie to face him, brushed her lips with his own. 'I just never imagined...'

He shook his head and kissed her mouth again. 'Come? Please.'

'Yes.' Josie linked her arms around Matthew's neck and nodded. 'Of course.'

Josie awoke to crisp skies and a sparkling frost. She leant her elbows on the sill of her bedroom window and stared out at the magical scene with a smile of pure joy.

It was perfect. Life was perfect. She loved Matthew. He wasn't involved with Kathryn. He wanted her as much as she wanted him. They were going to spend the day together.

Of course there were complications—what was that saying? The path of true love never runs smoothly? Well, she could cope with whatever obstacles she might have to face in the future. Just thinking about what Josh and Abbie had endured was enough to give her all the courage she needed.

She zipped through the shower, dressed herself at speed in warm layers—a black cashmere jumper, blue jeans, a fleecy orange jacket and practical leather boots—and was out of the house, heading for Harcombe Hall in her battered car, within the hour.

She refused to worry about coming face to face with Kathryn. Whatever she had said last night on the phone, it was not something she proposed to dwell on. Grief, jealousy—both were powerful emotions, ones that could twist and distort even the strongest characters. Kathryn had suffered, was still suffering. Now Josie knew the circumstances she would be better equipped to deal with the situation at Harcombe Hall—at least she hoped she would.

The tall iron gates were open. Josie turned her car off the main road and drove slowly up the tree-lined drive. The sun glinted magically through the skeleton of branches. There was the satisfying sound of gravel crunching under the tyres, the crisp, fresh smell of frost in the air. Instinctively Josie glanced towards the grassy bank on her left—far too early for the snowdrops to be visible yet, but in a couple of months they would be there, carpeting the whole area, an early promise of spring....

Josie inhaled a deep, calming breath as the house came into view. It was difficult trying not to feel as if she were coming home. So many hopes and desires whirring frantically around inside her head. *Calm down!* Josie told herself. *Don't think of any of that now.* She brought the car to a halt beside Matthew's gleaming vehicles and closed her eyes for a moment, forcing oxygen deep into her lungs.

The sound of knocking close at hand startled her. She clutched a hand to her chest and opened her eyes. Abbie, rosy-cheeked, with a red woollen hat on her head, was grinning at her through the car window.

'Hello, scamp!' A blast of cold air gushed into the car as Josie wound down the window. 'You're up bright and early!'

'Daddy said you were coming this morning. I've been waiting and waiting. Will you be playing with us today?'

'Of course!' Josie opened the car door and got out, smiling brightly down at Abbie's beautiful face. 'What do you want to do?'

'All sorts!' Abbie thrust her small hand into Josie's. 'You can teach us some new games.'

'What about hide-and-seek?' Josie reached in and pulled her leather haversack from the car. 'It's not new, but it's great fun. We'll ask Josh, shall we—and...and Daddy—if they'll play too? And Kathryn, if she wants,' Josie added, conscious of the need to try and do what was right.

'Hi!' Matthew, looking as ruggedly handsome as ever, dressed in jeans and a chunky ivory-coloured sweater, strode towards Josie with a look in his eyes and a smile of welcome that sent her heart into overdrive. 'You're nice and early,' he murmured, kissing her briefly but gently on the mouth. 'I'm glad.'

'I couldn't sleep,' Josie confessed, nerve-ends tingling at the sudden proximity of his body, at the feel and the taste of his mouth on hers. 'You're lucky I didn't turn up here at three in the morning!'

'I could have coped with that.' Matthew's voice was husky as he looked down into Josie's face. 'You know I could.'

'*Yes...*' She felt as if she was in a trance, a dream. She struggled to drag her eyes away from Matthew's mouth. She wanted him to kiss her—again and again and again... When he was this close, looking at her with a gaze that spoke so strongly of desire and need...

'Josie's going to play hide-and-seek with us!' Abbie's small voice hardly broke the spell, but it did remind them both that they weren't alone.

'Is she, now?' Matthew glanced down at Abbie and lifted her into his arms. 'That will be fun. Abbie's been watching at the window for the last half an hour—haven't you, sweetheart?'

'Put me down, Daddy,' Abbie instructed, wriggling free. 'I want to go and tell Josh Josie's here!'

'Full of energy, isn't she?' Josie murmured, with a smile, watching as Abbie scampered back towards the house. 'You must be worn out by the end of the evening.'

'Oh, not so you'd notice—I try and pace myself,' Matthew added with sparkling eyes. 'I'm usually longing for adult company, though—a particular adult's company,' he added, in a voice that was darkly seductive. He lowered his dark head towards Josie's and dropped a kiss upon her lips. 'Something tells me this is going to be a day that's full of temptation,' he murmured huskily. 'Are you ready for it?'

'What?' Josie's smile was light. 'The day, or the temptation?'

'Both.' Matthew's expression was pure seduction. He ran his fingers along the zipped edges of Josie's fleecy jacket, and then tugged her close. 'I've never been very good with temptation,' he drawled. 'How about you?'

A treacherous vision pierced Josie's thoughts suddenly: Matthew, strong, masculine, alone. And Kathryn, grieving, beautiful, in need of comfort. Wanting him. How many men would be able to resist? He had just said he wasn't good with temptation, and even though she knew he had been referring to her in that instant...

'What's the matter?' Matthew's dark brows drew together in a slight frown.

'Oh, I was just thinking...about Kathryn. She won't want me here, will she?' Josie added quickly. 'Things might get...awkward.'

'Don't look so apprehensive, sweetheart. She's not a dragon, just a very unhappy woman. And even if she was a dragon, I'd defend you anyway.' He struck a suitably comic pose. 'St Matthew—defender of this beautiful maiden!'

'You know, underneath all that suave sophistication you're still mad!' Josie announced, laughing.

'This is true.' Matthew's mouth curved into a heart-stopping smile. 'I thought I'd lost it for a while, but now you're around my crazy streak is coming back with a vengeance!'

Josie raised her brows. 'Thanks very much!'

'You know what I mean,' Matthew delivered huskily. 'Don't you...?' He kissed her then, long, slow, exploring her softly parted lips with his own, increasing Josie's desire as his tongue invaded the moistness of her mouth, as he held her close, one hand caressing her hair, the other sliding down the length of her body. 'Temptation,' Matthew whispered, against the heated skin of her throat. 'The sweetest and the cruellest of things. I don't seem able to stop kissing you,' he drawled, as his sensuous mouth descended yet again. 'Dreadful, isn't it?'

Josie wound her arms around his neck and smiled up at the crisp blue sky. 'Criminal,' she agreed happily. 'Absolutely criminal!'

'Oh, I couldn't agree more!'

Josie's heart thudded painfully against her chest. She turned sharply, dragging her mouth away from Matthew's to stare at Kathryn, who had suddenly appeared and was standing just a few feet away.

'About what?' Matthew's tone was cool, measured. He

didn't seem in the least perturbed by her appearance. Josie glanced up into his face and saw that his eyes were watchful.

'It is a beautiful day, isn't it?' Kathryn's smile was as bright as the day, but even so Josie was glad of Matthew's reassuring strength, of the protective circle of his arms which were still linked around her body. 'I'm making coffee,' Kathryn added, in a voice which revealed no hint of malice or dislike, with an expression which showed only the slightest strain. 'I just wondered if either of you wanted one?'

'Thanks.' Matthew's smile was genuine. 'That will be nice. We were just about to come inside.'

They walked back to the house together, Kathryn as Josie had never seen her before: seemingly relaxed and smiling, showing no signs of antagonism at her presence. Maybe things weren't going to be as difficult as she had feared—she always had suffered from a too vivid imagination. All those worries which had kept her awake for most of the night, about emotional outbursts and dreadful scenes...

Josie smiled warmly as Kathryn stepped aside to allow her into the house, and felt much cheered by the other woman's response. She had probably been angry last night—Matthew had left the party prematurely, and she had definitely sounded as if she had had too much to drink. No one was perfect.

She released an inward sigh of relief. It looked as if everything was going to work out all right after all.

CHAPTER NINE

'I'VE been clearing out the outhouses.' Matthew, with Abbie on his lap, helped her to pull on her boots. 'It's about the only place free from builders and decorators at the moment. There's an old tree down not far from the house. I've sawn it up into sizeable chunks. It just needs splitting and carting away.'

'Daddy bought us wheelbarrows specially so that we can help!' Abbie announced, wriggling from his lap. 'Josh says he can carry more than I can, but he put too much in and all the wood fell out!'

'Oh, did it? Well, I'm....I'm new to all this, so you two are going to have to show me what to do. Actually, I don't think I want a drink, thanks. I'll just go outside and make the most of the fresh air.'

'Josie doesn't drink coffee,' Matthew informed Kathryn. 'Can you make her some tea instead?'

'Of course!' Kathryn's voice was velvety rich.

'No!' Josie shook her head. 'No, it's OK—thanks anyway. I'm not very thirsty. I think I'll just go outside and sit in the sun.'

'Everything OK?' Matthew came to join her some few minutes later, coffee mug cradled in one hand.

'Of course!' Josie looked into Matthew's handsome face, thought of the danger of wanting something—some*one*—too much, and then looked away again. 'Why shouldn't it be?'

'Kathryn's a little tense this morning, but she's trying her hardest to be nice,' Matthew murmured.

'Yes, I saw.' Josie smiled. 'I can't pretend I'm not relieved.'

'You shouldn't worry so much.' Matthew reached forward and cradled her cheek with his free hand, turning Josie

137

resolutely to face him. 'I want us to have a good day together. It's very important to me.'

Josie looked deep into his eyes. 'And to me,' she whispered. 'And to me...'

His kiss was everything she had ever wanted. Josie closed her eyes and gave herself up like a willing sacrifice as his warm mouth covered hers in a slow, seductive demonstration of sexual desire, which threatened, indeed promised, to go on and on—if it hadn't of been for the sudden interruption by Abbie and Josh.

'Hey! You were kissing!' Abbie informed them indignantly.

'We were.' Matthew, one arm still encircling Josie's waist, reached down and lifted Abbie up to join them. 'Do you mind if we were?'

She considered for a moment. 'No, but it's pretty yucky stuff. Are you Daddy's girlfriend?' she asked of Josie. 'Kathryn was once. I saw them kissing in our old house, when I was four. It was at a party, and Kathryn had a silvery dress. She's very pretty, isn't she?'

'Yes.' Josie managed a smile. 'Very pretty.' She didn't look at him, although she knew he was looking at her. She had been right before—about jealousy; it really was a difficult emotion to deal with. Just hearing that Kathryn and Matthew had kissed sent a shock wave of despondency spiralling through her body.

'Daddy hugs her sometimes—when she's been crying too, don't you?' Abbie's dark eyes looked into Matthew's face.

'Yes.' Matthew stroked a finger across Abbie's plump cheek, seemingly unperturbed by her revelations. 'And I hug you too, and Josh.'

'He's grumpy!' Abbie wriggled to be put down.

'I am not!' Josh glared at his sister.

''Course you're not!' Matthew ruffled Josh's hair affectionately. 'Now, what about a little work, then afterwards we can all have a game of hide-and-seek?'

The children were enthusiastic—even Josh—and both

ran off to get their wheelbarrows in preparation for the task ahead.

'I did say we went out a couple of times.'

'Yes, I know.' Josie forced an expression of smiling innocence. 'Why?'

He looked at her for a moment without replying, then said, with a slight shake of his head, 'No reason.'

The rest of the morning passed by in a blur of activity. The sun lifted everyone's spirits, and there was much laughter and chatting as Matthew split wood into chunks and Josie and the children carted it away in their respective wheelbarrows to be stored in the barn for the following winter.

Kathryn didn't put in an appearance, and Josie couldn't help feeling glad. Then guilty. This image of Matthew with Kathryn in a 'silvery dress' in his arms wouldn't completely vanish from her mind either—which was silly, because she knew it was all in the past. She really did.

Josie stood in the doorway of the barn, watching as he swung his axe high in the air before bringing it down expertly to slice through hefty rings of wood like a hot knife through butter, and told herself for the twentieth time not to dwell on something she could do little about.

'I'm thirsty!'

'So am I!'

'I'll get us all a cold drink, shall I?' Josie dragged herself out of her reverie and smiled brightly at the children. 'You deserve a rest. You've worked very hard, both of you. Matthew couldn't have done all this wood-chopping without you two.'

'And you.' Josh, standing by Josie, looked up at her and smiled shyly.

Josie's heart went out to him; he looked so vulnerable in that moment: brave and forlorn and sad. 'Thanks.' She put an arm around his young shoulders and gave a squeeze. 'We're a pretty good team, aren't we?'

'Will you be with us for a long time?'

'Today? Oh, I should think until after lunch.'

'No, I meant…with Matthew.' Josh's gaze was assessing. 'You know,' he added a little awkwardly.

'Oh!' Josie felt herself colour slightly. She glanced towards Matthew, who had long ago discarded his sweater and was now in the process of pulling off his plaid shirt to reveal a pristine white tee-shirt underneath, and a torso inside that which was clearly in the peak of condition. The muscles of his arms flexed noticeably as he continued to work, and for a moment the sight of such glorious strength found Josie caught, mesmerised by the sight of him.

He must have felt her eyes upon him, for Matthew turned in the next moment and threw a crooked smile in Josie and Josh's direction. 'Everything OK?'

'Fine!' Josie called, her arm still around Josh's shoulders. 'I was just about to go and get us all a drink.'

'Good idea!' Matthew wiped the back of his hand across his glistening brow. 'Make mine a large one. After that we'll stop, and play those games.' Dark eyes sparkled mischievously. 'It's the only thing that's kept me going!'

'You do like Matthew, don't you?' Josh asked quietly. 'You must do, or you wouldn't kiss him so often.'

'Bit of a give-away, isn't it?' Josie agreed. She released a steadying breath. 'It's difficult to predict the future. All sorts of things can happen, good and bad—you and Abbie know that,' she added gently. 'But I hope so, Josh.' Josie turned and smiled down at the boy. 'I really do hope Matthew and I are together for a long time.'

'And me.' His smile was worth a lot. He pulled away then, as Abbie approached with her wheelbarrow, and began to help her load more wood.

Josie walked towards Matthew, venturing into the sawdust-strewn area littered with logs that still had to be taken to the outhouse. Matthew had stopped work and was watching her closely.

'Josh OK?'

'Yes, he's fine.' Josie beamed, conscious of the sexy vitality in his gaze. 'He likes me!'

'Of course he likes you.' Matthew's mouth curved. 'Did you ever doubt otherwise?'

'I hoped he did, but it's nice to have it confirmed.'

'Everyone likes you,' Matthew informed her, his gaze full of sensual vitality. 'Very much.'

Not everyone, Josie thought, but she refrained from stating the obvious. 'The children have been working very hard,' she murmured. 'I half expected them to give up after a couple of minutes, but they didn't.'

'You made a game of it.' The tone of Matthew's voice clearly showed his approval. 'They liked that. So did I.' His eyes held her face as she looked back at him, for a long, heart-melting moment. 'You're a very clever, beautiful woman,' he murmured huskily. 'I thought working like a maniac might relieve me of some of the pent-up desire which is racing round my body, but you know what?'

'What?' Josie whispered, mesmerised by the intensity of Matthew's gaze.

'It hasn't.' His mouth curved into a seductive smile. 'Do you think I ought to go throw myself in the stream to cool off?'

'And muddy that beautiful white tee-shirt?' Josie's expression was teasing. 'Have you forgotten the stream's only about ten centimetres deep?'

'Stay with me tonight.'

Josie's heart leapt. 'Here?'

'Where else? And before you mention her name, no, I haven't forgotten about Kathryn. But at this moment in time you're all I can think about.'

'And there's the children,' Josie reminded him softly, conscious of just how much she wanted to say yes to his proposal.

'And there's the children,' Matthew repeated flatly. He released a breath, dragging a hand through his shiny dark hair. 'I know! I know! I'm being selfish. It's just—'

Josie placed a hand over his, revelling in the touch of his skin beneath her slender fingers. 'I want you,' she murmured, 'as much as you want me—more so.'

Matthew's mouth curved into a crooked smile. 'Not possible,' he informed her steadily.

'But we have to give it time,' Josie continued.

'You mean Kathryn?'

'And ourselves too.'

'Not too much time.' Matthew dropped the axe he was holding to the ground. His movements had a sudden predatory aspect to them. 'Neither of us is made of stone,' he murmured, watching her face closely for reaction. 'There's only so much flesh and blood can stand.' His free hand slipped beneath the edges of Josie's jacket and roamed provocatively over the outline of her breasts.

'*Matthew!*' Josie gasped his name aloud.

His mouth curved. 'See?' he drawled, smiling. He dropped a kiss onto her lips, looked at her closely for a moment, then lowered his mouth once again.

'Hey!' Abbie, standing beside them with hands on hips, was looking up at them indignantly. 'You're kissing *again!*'

'I'll go and get us that drink.' Josie looked on happily as Matthew scooped Abbie into his arms with a growl and swung her high into the air. 'Then afterwards we can play hide-and-seek, like we promised.'

Inside the house, all was quiet. Josie opened a cupboard and pulled out glasses and a jug, before setting them on a tray. She wondered where Kathryn was; both cars were still in the driveway, so she couldn't have gone far. It was such a lovely day, maybe she had gone for a walk.

An odd noise found her hesitating with her hand on a kitchen drawer. A desperate noise, a cross between a wail and a sob, broke the silence suddenly. Josie hesitated a moment as the sound continued, then made her decision. She slipped off her boots and padded across the kitchen towards the hallway.

The sound of crying greeted her immediately. Heart-wrenching sobs, punctuated by wails of frustrated anger. Josie hesitated some more, uncertain whether now would be a good time to try and make peace. She retreated, then stopped and retraced her steps. She couldn't just leave her to cry all by herself. Should she get Matthew, or try and help Kathryn herself?

Josie's legs were slightly unsteady as she ascended the stairs, but she forced herself to push on, drawn by the misery of Kathryn's crying. She knew what it was like to lose someone you cared about; Sheila's death had left her bereft for months. If she could just make some sort of contact, talk to her, show her that she was willing to be friends, that things didn't have to be quite so bad between them, then maybe she'd be able to help.

Kathryn was in the first bedroom—a large, well-appointed room, with a magnificent four-poster bed, draped with material in a soothing mint-green colour. Josie hesitated at the open door. Kathryn was sprawled face-down on the bed, her long, luxurious hair spread over the counterpane, which was being gripped and twisted between elegant fingers.

She stopped writhing when she saw Josie in the doorway, but didn't get up. 'Come to gloat?' she asked rawly.

Josie frowned and shook her head. 'No, of course I haven't,' she murmured softly. 'I heard you crying and I thought—'

'That you'd really like to rub salt into the wound? Well, forget it! My wounds are painful enough as they are!' Kathryn raised herself to a sitting position and wiped her face with the back of her hand.

'Please! Let me help you, let me be your friend. Matthew's told me what you've all been through, and I do understand how hard everything is for you just now—'

'You understand nothing! Nothing!' Kathryn repeated in harsh tones. 'The two of us were doing fine until you came along!' she added. 'Just fine!' She rose from the bed and walked to a dresser, pulling tissues from a drawer to wipe her eyes. 'He's always had a weakness for young girls— you do know that, I suppose? Out in South America he had no end of brief relationships with pretty young things.'

'Kathryn, please—!'

'Please what?' Her look was full of sudden spite. 'Please

don't make things awkward for everyone—so that the course of true love can run smooth? He has declared his undying love, I presume?' Kathryn's gaze was all-seeing. 'Oh, dear!' Her mouth curved into a triumphant smile when Josie didn't reply. 'He hasn't. What a shame!' she added, with sarcastic sweetness. 'In that case you really are on rocky ground!'

Josie inhaled a steadying breath. She tried to remember that Kathryn had recently lost someone she loved, that a mixture of grief and jealousy were making her talk this way, but it was difficult. 'Look...' She worked hard at keeping her voice level. 'I understand how you feel. I know what it's like to lose someone you care about...but speaking this way, taking your anger out on me—or Matthew— isn't going to help—'

'You know how I feel?' Kathryn turned from the dresser, dark eyes flashing, waving her fist in Josie's direction like a weapon. 'How dare you? How dare you?' she repeated, almost beside herself with anger.

'Matthew and I...' Josie swallowed with difficulty. She hated confrontations—especially as bad as this. 'He cares about me—'

'Well, I'm the one living with him in this house!' Kathryn replied quietly. 'And I'll fight to keep it that way. You'd do well to remember that!'

It was no use. Arguing wasn't going to get either of them anywhere. 'I...I didn't mean to make you more upset than you already are,' Josie murmured. 'I'd better go.'

'Yes!' Kathryn replied, almond-shaped eyes boring into Josie's face like hot coals. 'You'd better!'

'Everything OK? What did you do, fly to Spain yourself for the oranges? I was just about to come inside to see what you were up to!' Matthew removed the tray from Josie's grasp and placed it onto a nearby chump of wood. 'Kids! Drinks!' he called.

'Great! Chocolate biscuits!' Josh's face lit up at the sight of the chocolate-covered digestives.

'I hope you don't mind,' Josie murmured, glancing at Matthew, who had already downed an extremely large glass of orange juice. 'I thought the children would be hungry.'

'Mind?' He raised a dark brow and smiled quizzically. 'Why should I mind? Hey!' He caught her arm as she tried to turn away. 'What's the matter? Has Kathryn been—?'

'No!' Josie forced a smile, and picked up a glass with a slightly unsteady hand. 'No, of course not! I'm fine!' She widened her smile—convincingly, she hoped. 'Now, are we going to play hide-and-seek, or not?'

The children loved every minute of it. The traditional old games don't lose their appeal, Josie thought, as yet another shout of delight travelled on the crisp winter air. Josie peeped around the side of the barn. Josh, successful this time, was looking flushed and triumphant, standing by the mark—a rusty, old-fashioned water pump, situated in the courtyard—which Matthew was supposed to be defending.

Kathryn was playing. Matthew had asked if Josie would mind, and after firm reassurances from herself that she didn't—not in the slightest—he had gone into the house and emerged, after a revealing length of time, with a blotchy-faced and distinctly subdued Kathryn by his side.

Josie didn't want any more conflict, and was relieved the nature of the game meant that there was hardly any direct contact between herself and Kathryn.

'Gotcha!' Josie started in surprise as Matthew, approaching silently from behind, encircled her waist with strong hands.

'Oh, goodness!' Josie let out a rush of breath, and clutched her heart. 'You frightened the life out of me!'

'Should have been on your guard!' Matthew turned her around to face him with a smile. 'Very lax!'

There was another shriek of delight. Both Josie and Matthew peered around the corner of the barn, watching as Abbie scampered from behind a tumbledown stone wall to join her brother at the pump. 'You were saying about being lax?' Josie murmured humorously.

'I need help.' Matthew tugged Josie out into the open. 'Just Kathryn to find—'

'No...I'll stay here with Josh and Abbie,' Josie replied quickly. 'You look for her alone; she'll appreciate that.'

'That's what I'm afraid of.' Matthew's mouth twisted into a crooked smile. 'OK, but don't move!' he ordered, with mock severity. 'And don't forget...' dark eyes sparkled sensuously '...you're my prisoner. I'll deal with you later!'

'She's in the barn!' Abbie whispered to Josie, when Matthew was out of earshot. 'I saw her go in there.'

'Oh, I see.' Josie followed Matthew's progress around the courtyard. 'Do you think she'll be found?'

'Oh, yes!' Abbie sounded full of confidence. 'Daddy's a very clever man, and Auntie Kathryn's a bit silly, isn't she, Josh?'

'*Abbie!*' Josh threw his sister an irritated look. 'Shut up!'

'Why? You're always saying she is!' she replied. 'Why do I have to shut up just because you say so—?'

'Hey! Come on!' Josie draped an affectionate arm around each child's shoulder. 'Let's not get cross with each other. We've had a lovely morning, and we don't want to spoil it, do we?'

'He's gone into the barn,' Abbie announced, darting away and then back again. 'I told you Daddy would find her!' She smiled gleefully at Josie, neat, even white teeth like a row of seed pearls in her mouth. 'I'm going to play a trick on them!'

'Oh, yes?' Josie smiled absent-mindedly. She knew it was silly, but after all that Kathryn had said the idea of the two of them alone together in the barn didn't exactly fill her with a great deal of joy. Not that she lacked trust in Matthew. It was just...well, loving someone *so* much, hardly daring to believe that they cared for you too—it made a person vulnerable, sensitive to the danger of losing him, joyously happy but at the same time secretly petrified that something should happen to take that happiness away. 'What sort of trick?'

'You'll see!' Abbie ran across the courtyard and around the corner towards the barn.

'Abbie, wait!' Josie glanced at Josh, who lifted his slender shoulders in a shrug.

'She's probably going to do something stupid,' he informed Josie conversationally. 'Last week she climbed to the top of one of the builder's ladders and then couldn't get down. Matthew had to climb up and get her.'

'Oh, goodness! Did she?' Josie glanced in the direction of the barn. 'She's a bit of a character, your sister, isn't she?' Josie flashed blue eyes at Josh. 'In that case we'd better go after her. Come on! I'll race you!'

Josie arrived a deliberate second behind Josh at the barn, but found herself disgustingly out of breath. She bent over, hands on knees, and made a silent promise to get in better shape before spring. 'It's all right,' she murmured to Josh, lifting her head, watching as Abbie crept theatrically around the walls of the old stone barn. 'She's only playing. She probably wants to jump out and scare the living daylights out of both of them.'

Josie, not wanting to intrude on Abbie's fun, walked over to an old horse trough, perching on the edge of the rim. She raised her face to the warming rays of the sun, then glanced back at the barn.

The door of the barn was only partially open, but it was enough.

And then, there they were. A moment caught, as if on celluloid. Not kissing—not in that moment—but close, looking into each other's eyes, a split-second glimpsed through the doorway of the barn: the two of them kneeling amongst the straw.

His hands were on her shoulders. At the sight of Kathryn and Matthew together, every uncertainty and fear that Josie had ever had rose to the surface to haunt her.

Nothing to worry about! Don't read more into it than there is! Don't! But when Josie shifted her gaze, and saw the embarrassed expression on Josh's face, she knew it was going to be difficult believing her own thoughts.

She looked away quickly, finding great interest in the moss and lichen that adorned the stone trough, trying to breathe calmly, to think of other things, as determined as she'd ever been not to allow Kathryn's hurtful words, the vision of the two of them together, to sully her hopes and dreams.

'Game over! Time for lunch?' His voice sounded wonderful, deep and smooth, with a gravelly undertone which always sent Josie's heart into overdrive. 'Josie?'

She looked up and managed a smile. 'Yes. That would be nice.'

'Kathryn?' Matthew glanced back towards the barn. Josh and Abbie were throwing bundles of straw at each other and Kathryn was watching with a faraway look on her face. 'Are you going to join us?'

She came over, straw still clinging to her long, slender legs. 'Join you for what?' she enquired, with a remarkably easygoing smile which, astonishingly, seemed to include Josie.

'Lunch?' Matthew sat beside Josie on the stone water trough but made no move to touch her, glancing up into Kathryn's face. 'Or have you other plans?'

'I do, as it happens.' Kathryn's smile, Josie thought, was now just a little strained, but her voice and whole demeanour were in such total contrast to the way she had been earlier, Josie had trouble reconciling the two. 'In fact,' Kathryn added, 'I must go inside and get changed or I'm going to be late. I'll just say goodbye to Josh and Abbie.'

Josie watched her walk back across towards the barn in a daze. What on earth was going on in that beautiful head of hers? It was almost as if the awful scene in the bedroom hadn't taken place.

'Hungry?' Matthew turned to Josie with a smile.

'Mmm.' Josie's reply was vague. 'A little.'

'Only a little? I'm starving.' He stood up, stretching his arms above his head. 'My stomach thinks my throat's been cut.'

'It's all that physical work you've done this morning,'

Josie replied quietly, her gaze unavoidably drawn by the masculine power of his frame. 'You'll probably ache like mad in the morning.'

'Will I?' Matthew stood before her, hands on hips. His mouth curved into a sensuous smile. 'Would you like to hang around and find out for sure?'

'I've already told you that's not a good idea!' Josie realised her reply had come out sounding more than a little sharp, but there seemed to be little she could do about it. Her whole body fizzed with tension. She felt confused, and unsure, and so unlike her usual happy, confident self, she wanted to cry. 'In fact,' she added, hardly pausing for breath or thought, 'I think maybe I should go home straight after lunch.'

'Why?'

Why indeed? Matthew's expression was serious, watchful—almost too gorgeously intent and sensuous to take. Almost. Josie tried to avoid his searching gaze, but he gave her no option other than to look into his eyes as he leant towards her and tilted her chin with one uncompromising hand. 'Tell me,' he commanded.

'Tell you what?' Josie whispered, playing for time.

'You look unhappy suddenly.'

'No, It's just...' She struggled for a reply, conscious of Matthew's watchful gaze. She thought about mentioning the fact that she had glimpsed the two of them in the barn, but hastily rejected the idea as soon as it had entered her head. What could she say? Nothing that wouldn't make her sound insecure and juvenile—*I saw you in the barn with your hands on Kathryn's shoulders. You were looking into her eyes. I thought...* What had she thought? That they were lovers? That was the bottom line, wasn't it? That was her fear. Why couldn't she just admit it? Josie inhaled a ragged breath. Because if she allowed thoughts like that to take hold, she'd go crazy, that was why. The two of them together in this house, with Kathryn feeling the way she so obviously did, was not something she wanted to dwell on.

'You know I want to make love to you,' he murmured huskily. 'Very much. Is that such a crime?'

A thrill of awareness zipped through Josie's body. The sound of his voice, the touch of his hand on her skin—simple things like that and her thought processes seized up.

'You don't seem too certain.' Matthew's tone was a little terse. 'No reply?'

'No, I—!'

'I'm off now!' Kathryn called, interrupting Josie's hasty denial. 'Bye, everyone!'

'Have a nice lunch!' Matthew's eyes didn't leave Josie's face. 'So, do you want to tell me what's bothering you?' he asked quietly.

'Nothing.' She shook her blonde head decisively, thought about the scene she had witnessed in the barn and made a determined effort to dismiss it. 'I'm sorry for snapping just now,' she added. 'Forgive me.'

'There's nothing to forgive.' Matthew crouched down on his haunches in front of her, resting both hands on her knees in a familiar, intimate gesture. 'If I'm pressurising you into doing something you're not ready for,' he added, looking deep into her eyes, 'then I'm the one that should be apologising.'

'Oh, Matthew!' Josie whispered. 'You're not—not at all...'

She held him fiercely as they kissed, aware of the desire building inexorably through her own body, sensing the control that Matthew was having to exert as his mouth moved over her parted lips, conscious of the children close at hand, of their own mounting desires which desperately needed to be assuaged.

'We can't go on like this,' Matthew all but growled as they extricated themselves from each other's arms. 'I've never wanted a woman so much in all my life as I want you,' he told her huskily. 'Don't!' He extended a hand and forestalled Josie from stretching up and lifting her hair away from her face with both hands. 'Every gesture is torture,' he murmured with a smile, 'and that one more than most. You look like an angel, and yet...' He released a long drawn-out breath.

'What?' Josie looked up at him, a smile hovering on her lips.

'I long to do the most wicked things with you,' he told her sensuously. 'Is my soul beyond redemption, do you think?'

'Possibly. Probably!' Josie replied. 'What sort of things?' she added, with a teasing smile.

It mattered that he did things right, that he didn't jump in with both feet and ruin the situation. She wasn't like the other women he had known—if 'known' was the right description. And thank God for that. Thank God for finding her...

They walked back to the house together, all holding hands, the children sandwiched between them, swinging and jumping over the uneven ground as they went.

'I've lots of ideas for the gardens,' Matthew commented, as they negotiated a rickety gate which led from the courtyard through to the side entrance of the house. 'But I'm open to any ideas. I'm going to have to replant the orchard.' Matthew stopped and pointed westward, to some distinctly gnarled old trees that had clearly seen better days. 'Bit of a shambles at the moment, isn't it?'

'Yes.'

'And there's the grounds around the house, of course. They'll be the priority. The building work is almost completed. I thought I'd wait a few months until I have the rest of the house decorated—time to get a feel for the place— but in the meantime I'd like to concentrate on getting the gardens up to scratch.'

'Oh...yes...' Josie thought of all the evenings she'd spent with paper and pencil and a pile of gardening books at her side. 'Good idea...' She walked on, conscious of the mass of insecurities that always rose to haunt her when she thought about the future. Too much to hope for—that she would be a part of Matthew's plans…

'Sorry.' His voice, when he next spoke, was clipped. 'I didn't mean to bore you—ramshackle houses and over-grown gardens aren't your thing, are they?'

Josie couldn't help feeling hurt. 'What makes you say that?' she asked quietly. But Matthew hadn't heard. She watched as he chased Josh and Abbie through the long grass towards the house, and wondered what he would say if he knew the truth about herself and her beloved Harcombe Hall.

CHAPTER TEN

'WAS the food that bad?'

'No…of course not.' Josie rose from the table, plate in hand. 'You do a mean roast chicken.' She bent to the dishwasher and began to stack the plates. 'I just wasn't very hungry, that's all.'

'Are you feeling OK?' Matthew threw Josie a searching glance. 'I'll do this. Go and sit down.'

'Actually, I have got a bit of a headache.' Josie smoothed a hand across her brow. 'All that activity this morning,' she added lightly, 'accompanied by the merry chatter of children. I'm obviously not used to it.'

'There are some tablets upstairs in the bathroom cabinet.' Matthew put down the dish he was holding and began to move towards the door. 'I'll fetch them for you.'

'No, I'll get them,' Josie replied. 'I need to use the bathroom anyway. 'Besides, ' she added playfully, 'I wouldn't want to drag you away from all of this.' She surveyed Matthew and the messy kitchen with a grin. 'You must have used every dish and plate in existence!'

'*We* must have… ' Matthew picked up a towel and flipped Josie across the backside with it. 'I'll be sure to save you the greasiest dish so you don't feel left out.' He picked up a plate with a grimace and placed it into the already crowded dishwasher. 'Thank heaven Mrs Milton will be in again tomorrow. That woman is a saint and a miracle-worker.'

'Only the very best at my agency!' Josie replied flippantly.

Matthew took hold of Josie by the waist and tugged her close against his body. 'I'm beginning to see that,' he murmured, kissing her lightly on the mouth. 'I'll clear this lot up,' he informed her huskily, after a moment, 'and then we can spend some quality time together.'

Josie's mouth curved. 'Sounds interesting,' she murmured.

'I'm hoping so.' Matthew kissed her mouth again, then trailed his lips along the line of her throat. 'When the children ask to watch a video, it usually means they'll be engrossed for an hour or so.'

'Yes, I noticed those persuasive powers of yours!' Josie remarked lightly. 'Very subtle. Josh and Abbie really ended up believing that it was their idea. I'll have to be aware of that in the future—could prove to be very dangerous!'

Matthew's dark eyes gleamed seductively. 'I live in hope.'

Josie padded upstairs in her stockinged feet. The tension she had been feeling ever since she had spied Matthew and Kathryn in the barn in what was, she had determinedly convinced herself, an innocuous position, began finally to dissipate. Flirting was fun. She loved it when the two of them could laugh and joke together, when the furrows in Matthew's brow relaxed and disappeared and he revealed more of the light-hearted personality that was still so much a part of him.

Josie used the bathroom, and then washed her hands at one of the two matching basins. This room was wonderful, she thought, looking round: large and airy, white porcelain fittings with gold taps, and simple cream furnishings—understated, but shouting out good design and taste. Josie's gaze rested on the neat finishing touches—a light fitting in the shape of shell, a recessed shelf displaying piles of thick white towels along with expensive oils and lotions. Everything perfect.

She moved across to the cabinet which was hung over the far basin. So, whose good taste was this? Josie wondered. Kathryn's or Matthew's—or both? Had they spent numerous evenings together, sitting in front of the fire with colour charts and fabric samples, excitedly deciding on the way each room should look?

Josie suppressed the thought that she would probably have felt better if everything had been done badly. She opened the cabinet distractedly, her eyes searching the shelves for the headache tablets, trying not to dwell on the notion that she would have at least been able to draw comfort then—from the fact that the house needed her as much as she still needed it. It was so difficult, being here as an interloper instead of as owner. Every new coat of paint, every metre of freshly tiled floor came as a reminder of what she had lost.

Of course there was a wonderful, stupendous, mind-blowing possibility that she might, one day, be part of a family here, but she did not—not even in her weakest moments, like now—allow herself to dwell upon the glorious notion that Matthew might...that they might—

No! Josie shut her eyes tight for a moment. If she thought about it, then it wouldn't happen. Hoping and wishing too much for anything was the surest way to see that dream fail and disintegrate.

Josie opened her eyes and scanned the contents of the cupboard. Kathryn's presence in the household was evident. It came as a curious blow to discover the intimacies of her female possessions stacked on the same shelf as Matthew's shaving kit.

Josie ran her fingers across the bristles of an elegant-looking shaving brush and wished her things resided alongside his instead of Kathryn's. She released a long drawn-out sigh. The need to be close to him increased with every minute that passed. Her whole body ached with it, and seeing Kathryn's possessions wasn't helping the way she felt one little bit.

She plucked the headache tablets from the top shelf, and was just about to close the cabinet when she saw another similarly shaped packet, already opened, tucked innocuously behind a tin of shaving foam. She stared at it for a moment in dismay, her heart thudding in her chest as all her insecurities came rushing to the fore.

Josie shut the cabinet quickly, and jerked on the tap. She

didn't want to look at it because it meant sex—somewhere, with someone. And that someone hadn't been her.

The cold tap was stiff and awkward. Josie jerked harder, until she felt it give, and was suddenly and comprehensively engulfed in a stream of water as the gold top came away in her hand. She shrieked instinctively, trying to cover the fountain of water with her hands, but it spewed forth beneath her ineffectual fingers, soaking everything within range, including herself.

'Damn! My fault. I meant to tell you not to use this basin. The plumber's returning tomorrow morning to fix it.' Matthew, entering the bathroom at a pace, grabbed a nearby towel and threw it over the leak. 'Where's the top?' he asked, looking around.

'Here.' Josie thrust it into his hands, watching with relief as Matthew managed to screw it back into place.

'Sorry!' Josie shook her head, looking around at the water-splashed walls and surfaces. 'I've ruined your lovely bathroom.'

'Don't worry about it.' Matthew reached for another towel from the shelf and handed it to Josie with a smile. 'Nothing a mop and bucket can't handle.'

'I'll go and get it, shall I?' Josie began to move towards the bathroom door. 'Is it downstairs in the kitchen?'

'Yes, but that can wait. You're more important.' Matthew surveyed her with gleaming eyes. 'Have you seen the state of yourself?'

Josie glanced down at her clothes. 'Oh!' she murmured.

'Oh, indeed!' He took her gently by the shoulders and ushered her out of the bathroom. 'Come on. I'll find you something else to wear.'

He led the way into his bedroom—the same room that Kathryn had been crying in earlier that day—and began rifling through a few drawers. 'What would you prefer— an oversize pair of my denims, or something of Kathryn's? I'm sure she wouldn't mind you borrowing something.' Josie watched in dismay as Matthew went to a cupboard and pulled out a clearly feminine pair of dark woollen trousers from amongst a selection. 'We're a bit short of space at the moment, and Kathryn has got more clothes than she knows what to do with,' he murmured. 'She won't miss them, I can assure you.'

'No, it's OK.' Josie inhaled a sharp, irritated breath as she struggled to slide her legs out of her soaking jeans. 'Something of yours will be fine, honestly—I like a loose fit.'

'Do you need any help?' Matthew came towards her with a pair of denims and a tweedy woollen jumper. He laid them on the bed behind Josie and stood for a moment, watching as she continued to struggle. 'Sit on the bed,' he suggested. 'You're making it difficult for yourself, standing up.'

'I didn't want to get anything wet,' Josie murmured. 'It's OK!' She pulled off her jeans with a relieved flourish. 'I've done it now.'

'And your sweater.' Matthew picked up Josie's denims from the floor and waited until she had pulled the garment over her head. 'I'll take them down to the tumble dryer.'

It wasn't until she had given Matthew her clothes that she realised the vulnerability of her situation. Josie looked into Matthew's face and saw with a lurch of desire that he was aware of it too. Dark eyes slowly travelled the length of her body, scantily clad now in bra, briefs, and a matching scooped neck bodice.

They stood facing one another. Tension filled the room. Somewhere beneath them, the faint sound of a television could be heard. Josie watched the fall and rise of Matthew's chest, felt the painful thud of her own heart.

'I'd better go.' His voice was calm, but he made no move towards the door.

'I don't want you to.' Josie's voice was barely a whisper, but it was enough.

Matthew dropped the clothes he was holding onto the floor and came towards her. Josie looked into his eyes as he held her, and her body quivered deliciously at the sight of such obvious desire.

Their kiss was a sudden clash of mouths, a hungry, forceful need that swept them both up in a maelstrom of emotion and feeling. Josie held Matthew as fiercely as he was holding her, welcoming the rough, enticing touch of his fingers on her bare flesh as his hands roamed the length of her body. She longed to be free of the restriction of her clothes, yearned for the feel of Matthew's strength and power inside the very heart of her. Close. Intimate. Where it mattered.

He left her, but only briefly. Josie heard the click of the door, the sound of the key turning in the lock. She didn't want to think about her insecurities or fears—they didn't exist any more. The only thing that existed was this moment, this need, this love which swept through her body like an all-consuming flame.

She wanted to be claimed by him whatever the cost. She wanted to be his, for now...for ever...for always...

He laid her on the bed, kissing her deeply, the thrusting intrusion of his tongue no intrusion at all, but a welcome rehearsal of what was to come. Expert fingers explored beneath the bodice Josie wore, unfastening the catch of her bra without difficulty, pushing aside the lacy material to reveal the fullness of her breasts, which Matthew held and caressed, before lowering his mouth to suckle on each hardened nipple in turn.

'You are so beautiful,' he told her huskily. '*So* beautiful...'

She felt the hardness of him, the obvious strength of his desire. She watched as Matthew raised himself to a sitting position astride her body and began removing the layers of his clothing. His torso was solid. Josie reached up and ran her hands over the smooth brown flesh, aware of the power beneath her own fingertips.

A shriek floated up from below. The sound of the television flared and then died down, followed by a spell of childish howling.

Josie stared up at Matthew, eyes wide in dismay and disbelief. 'It's all right. I've locked the door,' he murmured, listening, as Josie was, to the continued sounds down beneath them. He touched her with gentle assurance. 'It's probably nothing, they'll sort it out in a moment.'

But they didn't. The howling continued unabated. Matthew raised his mouth from Josie's lips and swore succinctly.

'It's no good,' Josie whispered, sitting up, shaking her head, suddenly aware of how little modesty mattered when Matthew looked at her with such obvious desire. 'One of us is going to have to go down and see what the matter is.'

'For heaven's sake!' he growled, as cries of anger punctuated the air. 'What the hell has got into them? No, you stay there,' he instructed. 'I'll go!' Matthew moved from the bed, cursing softly as he went. He glanced back at a half-naked Josie and shook his head, inhaling and releasing a slow drawn-out breath as he did so. 'You'd better cover yourself up,' he suggested tersely.

He stood for a few moments in the middle of the room, hands on hips, the flat, rippling planes of his torso still in evidence, staring down at the floor in silent contemplation. 'OK!' he announced after a moment. 'OK!' he repeated, glancing back towards Josie, who was pulling the jumper which Matthew had laid out earlier over her head. 'I can do this. It isn't the end of the world, even though it feels like it.' He shook his head again, and threw Josie a smile laden with regret. 'It's just not our moment, is it?'

'Not quite.' Josie picked up Matthew's hastily discarded plaid shirt and threw it over to him. 'You'd better put this on,' she suggested, smiling, 'or the children might wonder exactly what you've been up to.'

'No, they won't; they're too involved in their own argument by the sounds of it.' Matthew looked at Josie.

'There'll be another time,' she whispered softly, reading his thoughts.

'Soon.' Matthew came towards her, kissed her, kissed her some more, dragged himself away, as their embrace threatened to become all-engrossing, and crossed towards the door. 'And that's not a request!' he added, eyes devouring Josie as he turned the key in the lock. 'It's an order!'

An order with which she would have been happy to comply, but there simply was no other opportunity for them to have time together alone. Josie tried to feel philosophical about the whole thing, but it was difficult when every look and touch from Matthew reminded her of what they had both failed to achieve.

'I'm going to go home.' Josie touched Matthew's shoulder. The children were settled now, and happier, waiting patiently for Matthew to read them both a story in front of the fire. 'I've got a busy day tomorrow and I need to get organised for it.'

His expression as he looked at her was enigmatic. 'OK.'

'You don't mind?' Josie queried.

'Would it make any difference if I did? No—' Matthew's smile was reassuring '—I understand. You get off and do what you have to do…' He lifted a hand and lightly stroked Josie's arm. 'Kathryn will probably be back shortly anyway. I'll phone you tomorrow after work. We'll have dinner—alone.'

'That will be nice.' Josie, conscious of her own reluctance to leave now that she had made her decision, hesitated by the kitchen doorway.

'I'll see you to your car,' Matthew murmured. 'Do you want to say goodbye to Josh and Abbie?'

'Of course!' Josie released a pent-up breath. 'You've put me in a flat-spin,' she confessed. 'I don't know whether I'm coming or going!'

Matthew kissed her mouth. 'Think of *my* predicament— I've got to concentrate on *Winnie the Pooh* in a moment!'

'They love you very much,' Josie whispered, wrapping her arms around Matthew's neck.

'Don't be upset.' Matthew drew Josie away from him a little, so that he could look into her face. 'They like you a lot. It's just that at certain times—'

'Yes, I know…' Josie nodded. 'They need you more than anyone.'

The sun had long since disappeared. Late afternoon, and the light was fading fast. Josie drove along the driveway without looking back—it was torturous enough leaving, without prolonging the agony, she thought, resolving to try and stay in as upbeat a frame of mind as possible, whatever the circumstances.

Just as she was approaching the iron gateway a familiar vehicle turned off the main road and sped along the drive towards her. There was precious little room on the overgrown track for two cars side by side, but Kathryn clearly wasn't bothered about that. The Range Rover sped towards Josie, who had to turn her steering wheel sharply to avoid a collision with the larger vehicle.

Kathryn.

Josie brought her car to an undignified halt and watched her in the rearview mirror as the Range Rover continued on its erratic journey towards Harcombe Hall.

Up one minute, down the next. A twisting, torturous path.

No matter how hard Josie tried, she couldn't help thinking about that packet in the bathroom cabinet.

CHAPTER ELEVEN

'WELL, somebody sounds as if they're in a good mood!' Susan placed a handful of buff-coloured files onto Josie's desk, along with some neatly typed letters. 'Not bad for first thing on a Monday morning. Festive season finally got to you, has it?'

Josie stopped humming and turned around quickly at the sound of Susan's voice. She had been staring out of the window at the rush hour traffic in a daze. 'Maybe!' she replied with an enigmatic smile.

Susan raised arched brows. 'That good was it—the weekend?'

'Oh, you know…pretty acceptable.' Josie thrust her hands into the pockets of her cashmere jacket and looked back at the window. She didn't trust her ability to keep her expression neutral—not when all she could think about was Matthew: the way it had felt to be in his arms, visualising the glory of his naked torso, the predatory expression in his eyes as he touched and kissed her. They had been so close to making love. Josie released a shaky breath. Even now…all these hours later—and she still felt the sharp ache of unrequited desire. Did Matthew feel it too?

'Would that be 'acceptable' as in 'glorious, wonderful, out of this world'?' Susan's voice was bright. She crossed the room and stood beside Josie at the window. 'Come on, madam!' Susan grinned, folding her arms in resolute manner. 'This is me you're talking to—the good friend who's been going out with the same man since she left college. I need some excitement in my life! You saw him, I take it— Matthew Jordan?' Josie nodded, trying unsuccessfully not to look too pleased with herself. 'And?' Susan's plump face was a picture of barely disguised interest. 'Look, I'm not asking for all the gory details or anything,' she added, still

162

smiling. 'Just a hint as to how things are progressing between you two.'

'We spent most of yesterday together, and it was…good,' Josie replied simply.

'Only good?'

Josie released a small breath. 'OK, better than good. But there were a few…complications.'

'Oh, I see.' Susan hesitated a moment, then added, 'You knew it was never going to be easy—'

'Tell me about it,' Josie murmured dryly.

'I've been wondering…' Susan's gaze was fixed on Josie's face. 'That woman who came in here the other day—she's not his wife, then?'

'No.' Josie shook her head and moved to her desk. She really didn't want to go into this right now. She picked up a pen and began to sign the letters Susan had placed on her desk.

'His sister?' Susan asked, almost hopefully, turning to straighten the contents of the out-file tray.

'No.' Josie's voice was neutral. 'Not his sister either.'

'But they *are* living together?'

Josie rummaged in a desk drawer for nothing in particular. 'For the time being—yes, but not in the way you mean. I was mistaken—about the nature of their relationship,' she added swiftly. 'Everything's going to be all right.'

'I see.' There was a moment of silence. For once, Josie thought, Susan was doing a remarkable job of thinking before she spoke—although *what* she was thinking wasn't exactly difficult to surmise.

'Look, it's a complicated situation,' Josie informed her swiftly, before she could state the obvious. 'I'm not pretending otherwise.'

'You love him, don't you?' Susan murmured.

Josie hesitated, but only for a moment. 'Yes. Yes, I do.'

'And he loves you?'

'Y-yes.' Josie twisted the pen over and over between her fingers. 'Yes, I think so.'

'But he hasn't said as much?'

'Not in so many words.' Josie met her friend's gaze. 'Susan please—!'

'I know! It sounds as if I'm prying—sticking my nose in where it's not wanted—and I am, but only because I'm worried about you! I know they say love is blind, but how can you be so naive?' She shook her auburn curls in frustrated amazement. 'They say the course of true love never runs smooth—and how can it, in your case, when a gorgeous, masculine hunk like Matthew Jordan is shacked up with a glamourous, beautiful woman like what's-her-name?'

'Susan, I've told you—it's not like that!'

'And you trust him to keep his hands off her, do you?' Susan persisted bluntly. 'You know, men often have the best of intentions, and I don't doubt that Matthew *wants* to be good, but when certain situations present themselves—'

'That's enough!' Josie rose from behind her desk. She couldn't cope with this right now—especially not from a friend whose judgement she usually trusted. 'I think perhaps you'd better get on with whatever it is you have to do!' She inhaled a steadying breath and glanced at her wristwatch. 'It's getting late, and I'm supposed to be at the opening of the Overton branch later this morning.'

'Oh, hell!' Susan frowned. 'I'm sorry! All that came out sounding... I didn't mean—!'

'It's OK.' Josie closed her eyes briefly, and then looked into Susan's troubled face. 'I know you didn't, but you must understand that I'm not a fool. Don't you think I'm aware of the dangers of the situation?' Josie released a taut breath. 'Hell! I spent most of last night worrying about them!'

'But why? If you're so sure Matthew and she aren't—'

'They're not.' Josie's voice was firm. 'Matthew wants *me*. He's made that much patently clear.'

'So you've slept with him, then?'

'*Susan!*'

'I'm sorry, it's just...' She released a breath. 'Look, if

things have got that far already, then forget what I just said about you-know-who. I was just trying to...to help, before you got in too deep.' Susan reached across the desk and touched Josie's arm lightly. 'I don't want him to hurt you, that's all. Surely you can understand that?'

'Yes.' Josie's voice was quiet. 'Yes, I can. But I'm a big girl now, and perfectly capable of taking care of myself. And I know Matthew a whole lot better than you do.'

'Of course.' Susan's smile was bright—too bright maybe. 'Forget I ever said anything.'

But of course it wasn't that easy.

Josie tried not to let the conversation with Susan upset her, but it was difficult not to dwell on it throughout the rest of the morning.

The opening at Overton of the latest branch of the employment agency was as well organised and satisfying as the others had been, but somehow her heart wasn't quite in the ribbon-cutting and speech-laden ceremony, and she hardly touched anything during the buffet lunch which followed.

She couldn't stop thinking about him. Her whole body ached with a longing which was quite unlike anything she had ever experienced before.

All she wanted was to be with Matthew.

Constantly.

Her mobile phone rang twice in the morning, and each time Josie's heart leapt. She made a special effort to go somewhere quiet, just in case he had somehow got hold of her number, and on both occasions it wasn't him. Just business. Like always.

By early afternoon, Josie had a splitting headache. She shook hands with the new manager—a capable, charismatic woman in her late forties—and left the Overton branch of her employment agency with a weary sigh of relief.

She had spotted a chemist's shop just off the high street on her arrival, so she left her car in the small car park at the back of the premises and walked the short distance, huddled inside her long camel coat, in order to buy some much needed aspirin.

The pavements were glistening with a recent fall of rain. The shops she passed were bright and welcoming, crammed full with shoppers and goods. It was almost Christmas! Josie smiled, despite her aching head, at the thought of what lay ahead—for the first time in more years than she cared to think of she would have someone special to share it with.

The chemist was tiny, old-fashioned. Almost empty. Clearly suffering from the competition of a larger, more up-to-date drugstore at the other end of the high street.

Josie stared absent-mindedly, waiting patiently on the pavement whilst an elderly shopper with a Zimmer frame departed at snail's pace. Through the shop's artificial snow-covered window, displaying a cheerful but rather limited selection of soaps and bath salts, she could see the till. The shop assistant, she noted, looked bored to tears. Josie's thoughts wandered back to the opening. She wondered if the Overton branch would reach its recruitment target on time, and discovered with her next thought that she didn't much care if it did or not.

Love. Somehow it made things that she had imagined were important seem not quite so important after all.

A pregnancy predictor kit was placed on the counter. Josie released a small sigh. She wasn't pregnant, but she wanted to be—so much. To be carrying Matthew's baby…Josie's heart flipped over in her chest. What must that feel like? She closed her eyes for a brief moment and imagined the wonder of it, glorious, special, magical…

When she opened them again, the pregnancy kit had been placed in a paper bag and money was being exchanged.

There was something about those long, elegant nails, the quality of the dark coat trimmed with fur, which made Josie look again, only harder this time. She peered through the fake snow and silvery tinsel of the window display, and a bolt of dismay shocked her to a standstill.

It couldn't be. *No! No, please!* a small voice screamed inside her head. *Don't let it be!*

But it was.

Kathryn.

Her first thought was that Susan had been right about temptation. Her second that she had to get away—*right* away. To allow Kathryn to see her in such a distraught state was unthinkable.

Josie swivelled round and cannoned straight into a mother with a pram, banging her shins painfully on the metal edge. 'Sorry!' She frowned and placed an apologetic hand on the woman's arm. 'I'm so, so sorry! I didn't see you.' She glanced into the pram, agonised by the sight of a tiny face and a knitted woollen bonnet.

A sob caught in her throat, and it was all she could do to stop from crying aloud. It couldn't be true. But even if Kathryn wasn't pregnant, it still meant…

Josie gasped a breath, paralysed by her worst fears—'what if's' that were too awful to contemplate.

'Josie!' Kathryn sounded startled. Josie stilled, gave herself a moment, and then turned reluctantly to face her.

'Hello, Kathryn,' she murmured shakily, her eyes drifting of their own accord to the package held tightly in Kathryn's hands. 'Fancy seeing you here.'

'Yes, I was just…' Her dark eyes pierced Josie's face. There was a moment's silence. 'You look upset,' she continued coolly. 'Something wrong?'

'No.' Josie gathered all her resources, and continued in a voice that sounded reasonably in control. 'I've just got a bit of a headache, that's all. I was just about to get some aspirin.'

'Quite a coincidence—our meeting like this.' Kathryn's voice was more composed now.

'Yes.' Josie wished her stomach wasn't churning quite so much; she felt dreadfully sick suddenly—which was ironic, wasn't it? She wondered if Kathryn felt the same way. 'I saw you…in the chemist,' she added stiltedly.

'Did you?' Kathryn raised an enquiring brow. 'Is that why you look so…shocked?' She glanced down at the package in her hands for a moment, and then looked back at Josie. 'Ah, now I see! You saw my purchase.' Her gaze was calculating. 'I told you I'd fight for him, didn't I?' she added coolly.

Keep calm! Keep calm! The small voice inside Josie's head was doing its best, but she refused to listen to it.

She stared at Kathryn, unable to speak, hardly able to think coherently. Then she ran. Anywhere. In any direction, losing herself amongst the hordes of people, not stopping until she had put distance between herself, the pregnancy kit and Kathryn.

She needed space—time to think, to sort it all out in her mind. Temptation. The word kept buzzing around in her mind. She should have known. Kathryn would have had no qualms about luring Matthew. She imagined any number of scenes: Matthew comforting a distraught Kathryn late at night, holding her, kissing her, one thing leading to another... She was incredibly beautiful, with a body that most men would die for—and she wouldn't have been frightened of flaunting that body, using it to get what she wanted...

Josie pressed a gloved hand against her face. Now, *now* she could allow herself to think about her worst fears. Words from Matthew's own lips came back to her—she heard his voice... *'I'm not very good with temptation...'* That was what he had said, and now, standing on the pavement, with hurrying shoppers all around her, she finally believed him.

Josie looked up. She was standing outside a travel agency. It seemed like a sign. She thought for a moment, then ventured towards the door and stepped inside...

She wasn't at home. She wasn't at the office. There was no doubt that her secretary was being evasive, if not downright tight-lipped about Josie's whereabouts.

Matthew rubbed a hand over his unshaven face. What on earth was going on?

Why hadn't she called him? He had tried the number of her mobile phone a thousand times, and still no reply. Why didn't she want to speak to him? What could have hap-

pened in such a short space of time to make her behave
this way?

A vision of Josie, lying beneath him just twenty-four
hours earlier, flashed with torturous clarity into his mind.
She was so…perfect. When he had met her, held her, kissed
her for the first time, it had been as if…as if the whole
world had fallen into place. As if everything made sense at
last.

Matthew pressed his forehead against the window pane
in the children's bedroom, and closed his eyes. She was
safe. Alive. Evidently her secretary was allowed to tell him
that much. But it wasn't enough.

He needed her. More than anything.

Where was she?

Money didn't bring happiness, Josie knew that well enough
by now, but at least it meant she could deal with her misery
in any way she chose.

Travelling to Brussels on the spur of the moment wasn't
exactly what she had had in mind this morning, but as soon
as she had discovered the next available flight from the
local airport she had taken it, because somehow it had
seemed the obvious thing to do.

Madness, perhaps. But infinitely preferable to the alternative: returning to her little house, struggling with the
thought of having to face the fact that Kathryn and
Matthew…

Of course there was the possibility that Kathryn was lying, that she herself had jumped to a horrendous conclusion,
but however hard she tried to be positive, the evidence
seemed just too overwhelming.

If Kathryn wasn't so determined to have him, if she
hadn't known they had once been together, if she hadn't
seen that moment in the barn, or the condoms in the cabinet, or if Susan hadn't voiced her own anxieties. *If, if, if*…

Josie felt the hot sting of tears beneath her eyelids as she
boarded the plane. She had no luggage, just her passport,
her credit cards, and herself. She would go away. She knew

she wasn't thinking straight, but she needed time to sort everything out clearly in her own mind. That she loved him was without doubt. Hurt pride was one thing; this crushing pain, like a lead weight inside her soul, was quite another. But that wasn't enough, was it—loving someone so much you thought you were going to die with the pain of it?

Josie sat staring into space, oblivious of her surroundings as the plane gathered speed and launched itself into the cold grey sky. *Matthew! Matthew! How could you do this to me?* The small voice inside her head was at work again. She felt so bad she wanted to wail aloud, but she didn't. She simply stared out of the window and thought about the possibility of Kathryn having Matthew's baby.

Her secretary was stubborn, that was for certain. Loyal too. Josie had gone away on some unexpected business. A sudden development. She did not wish to be contacted—not by anyone. That was all she knew, she told him, clearly annoyed at having to repeat herself for the umpteenth time, and Matthew, looking closely for signs of unease in her expression, saw only a thinly veiled hostility, and was inclined to believe what she said as the truth.

Two days of torment. Wondering about her. Trying to imagine what could have happened to make her behave in such a way.

Matthew stared, glassy-eyed, at the book he was supposed to be reading. He had never felt this way before, as if a part of him was missing. It had taken him some time to admit to the strength of his feelings, but now he understood. Absolutely.

'Go on!' Abbie placed a small plump hand on his arm. 'Why aren't you reading the next page?'

He loved her—with all his heart. He loved her...

'Sorry, sweetheart.' Matthew dragged himself back to the task in hand.

'You look sad,' Josh murmured. 'Is it the story?'

'No.' Matthew forced a smile. 'Not the story...' He flipped over the page. 'Now, where were we?'

Kathryn came into the bedroom. She had been subdued recently, thoughtful. He looked at her and saw something new in her face—a determined, resolute expression which made him pause, dark brows raised in query.

'I need to talk to you,' she said.

A week was too long. Two days had been bad enough. Silly to imagine that running away from her problems would solve anything. 'Out of sight, out of mind' might be applicable to some people, but certainly not to a man like Matthew Jordan.

She was miserable. She ached to be with him. She loved him.

She was coming home.

The house was just as she had left it. Untidy, gloomy, clothes on the floor, curtains still drawn in every room. Josie dumped her suitcase in the hall and stooped to pick up the post. Nothing interesting. Just bills and circulars, and a few Christmas cards from friends and distant relations.

No letter from Matthew, asking her forgiveness and declaring undying love.

Nothing.

The doorbell rang. Josie's heart leapt. She rushed to open it, nearly tripping over her recently acquired luggage in the process.

'Hi!'

It wasn't him. Depression weighed her down again like a dark, heavy cloak.

'Hello, Craig.' Josie struggled to find a smile. 'What do you want?'

'Can't a friend make a call without wanting anything?' His voice, Josie decided, sounded far too chipper in the gloom of her cold, dark house.

'Sorry!' She released a breath. 'I didn't mean to sound...well, you know. You surprised me, that's all. I've only just this minute returned.'

'Yes, Susan told me you were away.' Craig lifted an

eyebrow in knowing observation. 'Rather sudden, wasn't it?'

Josie was already regretting her decision to open the door. 'What was?'

'Your holiday.'

'I...I just felt like a break. Spur-of-the-moment thing.'

'To Brussels?' Craig's tone was sardonic. 'How curious.'

'It's a very attractive city, actually,' Josie replied briskly.

'Oh, I don't doubt that.'

Josie moved through to the kitchen. She didn't think she could endure another moment standing in the cramped, cold hall; she felt miserable enough as it was.

The lights, recessed beneath the wall cupboards, gave the kitchen a warm atmosphere, despite the definite chill in the air. 'Hell! It's cold!' Josie opened a cupboard and flicked the central heating switch, before lifting the kettle and filling it under the tap.

'I can't believe you just flew off without a word to anyone—very out of character!' Craig commented. 'Kathryn mentioned you'd gone—Matthew's been beside himself, apparently. She tried to convince him that it wasn't her fault, but he's been very difficult—practically accused Kathryn of driving you away, somehow, which is ridiculous, because, as I said to Katy, you're a strong woman; you know your own mind. It would take more than some silly misunderstanding between the two of you to have you flying off to Europe and abandoning everything. Of course, when she told Matthew her news, he was completely floored—not that I can blame him; I was rather floored myself!'

Josie looked at Craig in dazed fashion as she tried to assimilate all that he had said. His pale face was unusually flushed, and there was a bright, iridescent gleam in his eyes. 'Are you on something?' she asked. 'You're talking like...well, like—'

'Someone in love?' Craig grinned at Josie's incredulous

expression. 'I am *so* happy, Josie. So happy you wouldn't believe!'

'Actually, looking at your face right now, I think I would.' Josie murmured, managing a smile despite everything. 'But…' She hesitated, hardly able to bring herself to say the name, 'You mentioned Kathryn…' Josie shook her head. 'Sorry, Craig, but I'm feeling a little…worn out. What are you talking about?'

Craig came towards Josie and held her gently by the shoulders. 'Are you OK?' he asked. 'You look kind of…miserable.'

'I am.' Josie swallowed. Her throat felt tight, and she had to struggle to hold back the tears.

'Poor old thing!' Craig's voice was painfully jovial. 'The course of true love never quite runs smooth, does it?'

'Don't!' Josie dragged herself free of his hold. 'Don't say that!' she repeated, turning from Craig. 'This isn't a good time for me, Craig.' Josie rubbed a hand over her face. 'Surely you've worked that out by now?'

'Sorry. I know you've only just got back, but I was passing and I saw the light—OK.' Craig threw Josie a rueful grin. 'I came out of my way on the off chance that you might be back. I'm *so* excited, Josie, I can hardly think straight! It's Kathryn—!'

Suddenly she understood—or at least she thought she did. 'Oh, no!' Josie shook her head. Bad enough that she was being made to suffer by the woman, but Craig as well… 'Oh, no… Craig, I know she's beautiful, and you probably got some mad crush on her the first time you saw her or something, but—'

'More than a crush,' Craig smiled. 'I thought you knew.'

'Knew what?'

'That we've been…seeing each other—not in the conventional sense, maybe—we haven't been out publicly— but we have been spending time together—a lot of time.'

Josie's heart lurched in her chest—which was weird, because it had felt so dull and leaden lately, she'd honestly thought it was broken. 'What sort of time?' she asked cautiously.

'*Time* time!' Craig's mouth split into a mischievous smile. '*Wonderful* time.'

Josie's mind was beginning to race. 'I...I had no idea,' she murmured, hardly daring to allow herself to hope. 'You and Kathryn,' she repeated, just so that there could be no mistake. 'Is it serious?'

Craig lifted his shoulders. 'What can I say?' he answered lightly. 'Except I'm mad about her.'

'And does she...feel the same way about you?'

Craig's bright expression dulled, but only a little. 'We're getting there. I'm not a fool, Josie. I can see the incredulity in your expression, and at first...yes, I'll admit it was pretty much one-sided, and I know she came to me because...well, she had no one else. But now...' He inhaled a deep breath. 'Now, things are different.'

'How can you be sure?' Josie frowned. 'Craig...I don't mean to burst your bubble or anything, but—'

'She's going to have my baby.' Josie stared at Craig in astonishment. 'Well, aren't you going to say anything?' He sounded a little put out. 'Congratulations wouldn't go amiss, you know.'

'I'm sorry...' Josie rubbed a hand over her face. She felt exhausted, almost too tired to think straight. 'Congratulations.'

'I wanted you to be the first to know—well, actually you're the fourth, counting Kathryn, Matthew and myself—'

'*Matthew?*' Just the sound of his name made Josie's body tremble. 'He knows?'

'Yes, Kathryn wanted to tell him straight away. She's going to move out of the house. They talked, straightened out a few things.'

'Oh, Craig...!' Behind her, the kettle shrieked, announcing it had boiled, but Josie scarcely heard it. 'How do you...?' Josie hesitated. It was difficult forming the words—apart from anything else, she didn't want to hurt Craig's feelings.

'The baby *is* mine,' he informed her steadily.

'But Kathryn and…and Matthew.' Josie shook her head, hardly able to bring herself to say it. 'I saw Kathryn. She was in Overton on the same day as the opening.'

'Yes, she came with me.'

'With you?'

Craig smiled. 'I was at the opening too—remember?'

'Yes, but—'

'She said she bumped into you,' Craig continued, 'and you had a brief chat—'

'"A brief chat"…yes.' Josie spoke quietly, remembering.

Craig came towards her. 'She really is very sorry for the things she's said to you. Intimating the baby was Matthew's was unforgivable.'

'She told you she'd said that?' Josie placed a hand against her head and stared at Craig.

'Yes. Actually… Josie…' He looked uncomfortable for a moment. 'Kathryn's outside, sitting in the car. I said I'd come in first and pave the way. She really would like to speak to you.'

'About what?' Josie couldn't keep the bitterness from her voice. 'About the way Matthew can't keep his hands off her? Because that's the message she's been giving me. Sorry, Craig.' Josie glanced at him and shook her head. 'I don't mean to be—'

'It's the wrong message.'

Josie looked up sharply. Kathryn, dressed warmly in jumper, jeans and woollen jacket, was standing in the kitchen doorway. 'I want to apologise,' she announced swiftly. 'For the things I said, for the way I behaved towards you. I've been so…awful lately. After the accident…' Her bottom lip trembled noticeably. 'I felt so…angry. I tried to be strong, for the children's sake, but inside…inside I was a mess.' She shook her head. 'Looking back over the past few months…well, it isn't difficult to see now that I've been a little crazy.' Kathryn paused, her almond eyes steady on Josie's face. 'I've treated you badly. It's nothing personal—you were just in the wrong place at the wrong time. For me at least.'

An unhappy smile hovered on her beautifully painted mouth. 'You seemed so...so together, so untouched by tragedy. And you were an old friend of Matthew's. I suppose I was jealous.' She inhaled a steadying breath. 'No suppose about it. I *was* jealous. You can't have failed to notice that we haven't been getting along very well, and you two just seemed...perfect together. She paused. Josie could see her running over everything in her mind. 'I'd somehow got it into my head that there was a future for the two of us. It was something to cling onto, to work towards. Matthew's such a strong, capable man. I didn't see how I'd ever be able to get through everything without him. I thought I needed him, but I don't.' Her voice was firm. 'Not now.'

Kathryn glanced at Craig, and smiled hesitatingly, then looked back towards an ashen Josie. 'Matthew and I have never been lovers. He isn't interested—has never been interested. I know I've been horrible and I'm sorry...' Her voice broke slightly. 'Truly sorry.'

Josie hardly knew what to say. She watched as Craig took Kathryn in his arms and held her close. She felt so alone suddenly, so desperately alone...

'I've got to go.'

'To Matthew?' Craig lifted his head from Kathryn's shoulder.

'Yes.' Josie's reply was breathless. 'I can't believe I've allowed things to become so... I should have talked to him!' she added wildly. 'I've been so stupid!' Josie stared about her in utter anguish. *'Oh, Matthew!'* Her voice was barely a whisper. 'I should have trusted you.'

CHAPTER TWELVE

THE children had taken a while to get to sleep tonight. They sensed his unhappiness, he knew, even though he tried his best to be upbeat and cheerful whenever they were around.

Matthew carried the plate of chicken casserole, which Mrs Milton had left warming in the oven, to the sink. He wasn't hungry—would probably never be hungry again…

He had to stop this…this self-pity. Matthew stretched his arms above his head. His shoulders were aching like hell—his whole body was aching. Although that had little to do with too much physical exercise. He went to the utility room and slipped on some boots. The puppies needed checking on. He thanked the Lord that the weather had been bad enough today to keep the children indoors. Christmas Eve tomorrow, and after that he wouldn't have to keep them a secret any longer.

Josie watched, her heart beating wildly in her chest, as Matthew walked around the side of the house in the direction of the courtyard. It was cold. He had no coat on. She wondered where he was going.

She opened the car door quietly and got out. She was shaking so much she could hardly place one foot in front of another. *If he rejected her. If he told her everything was over between them…* It didn't bear thinking about.

There was a dim, reddish light coming from one of the outhouses. She could hear the low murmur of Matthew's voice.

Josie skirted the edges of the courtyard, hardly breathing as she got near to the doorway.

The light came from an infra-red lamp. There was a large mesh cage, with newspaper and feeding bowls, a cardboard box which had clearly seen better days, and Matthew, sitting on the floor, with two black retriever puppies in his arms.

She watched him for a long moment, gathering the courage to make her presence known. When she eventually spoke, her voice sounded strange and croaky. 'Matthew...'

He looked up at her. Dark, enigmatic eyes resting on her face. He didn't move or say anything, seemingly oblivious as the puppies wriggled and squirmed in his arms. Josie gripped the doorway; she could feel the roughness of the wood beneath her fingers. 'Hello...' she murmured, conscious of the silence between them. 'Aren't you...?' She gasped a ragged breath, tried to smile. 'Aren't you going to say anything?'

'What do you want me to say?' His voice was cool and steady, not angry or emotional. Josie's heart sank. Not anything.

''Hello' would be a start,' she replied lightly.

'When did you get back?' Matthew's voice was expressionless.

'This evening.'

'And you went to...?' Dark brows were raised in unsmiling query.

'Brussels.'

'Brussels,' he repeated, without emphasis. He glanced down at the puppies and then stood up and bent over to put them back into their cage. 'Not long now, and then they'll be in the house,' he commented neutrally, watching the two as they rolled around, paws all over the place, biting each other's ears in playful fashion. 'It's been difficult keeping the children from seeing them.'

'Yes.' Josie smiled wanly. 'I'll bet. They're going to love them,' she added, trying to sound upbeat. 'It's a wonderful idea.'

'I figured they needed something new to focus on— something special to love,' Matthew murmured. He looked across at her. 'We all need that.'

'Matthew...please—!' Josie ventured towards him, stopping before she got too close because he looked so cold and distant, and the idea of rejection now—when she needed him most—terrified the life out of her.

'I've been trying to get in contact with you,' he informed her.

'Yes, I know,' Josie replied miserably. 'I'm sorry.'

'I have no idea why you went away,' he murmured. 'Care to enlighten me?'

'I was...overwrought, mixed-up—'

'Not sure about us.'

'No!' Josie shook her head. Matthew's unflinching gaze was almost too much to bear. She hung her head. 'Well, yes, sort of,' she added.

'I see.'

'No, you don't!' Josie threw him an anguished glance, hating the cool, enigmatic tone of his voice. 'You don't see at all!' She dragged badly needed oxygen into her lungs. She felt almost faint with tension and fear—fear of losing him. 'Matthew, I'm sorry! I ran away and I shouldn't have. I've not been thinking straight.' Josie shook her head. Being this close, seeing the look in his eyes—the hurt, the coldness... 'You have no idea what it's been like—!'

'Haven't I?' His voice was like granite: hard, harder than anything she had ever known. Josie looked into his face and saw the anger simmering below the surface. 'You can stand there and say that to me?' He shook his head, a cold, disbelieving smile hovering at the edges of his mouth. Josie looked at his hands and saw that they were gripping the edges of the kennel so hard his knuckles showed white. 'I thought we were...' He shook his head. 'I thought we had a future together!'

'Matthew, please—!'

'For God's sake! Stop saying that!' Now the anger was clear—in the tone of his voice, the tough, uncompromising expression in his face. 'What the hell do you want from me? My forgiveness because you suddenly decided you had second thoughts about the two of us? Well, I'm the one who's sorry, but it just happens that I'm not in a very forgiving mood!'

'Matthew, it's not like that! I love you! I want to be with you!'

Ebony eyes pierced her face. 'Me or this house?'

'What?' Josie stared at him in amazement. This was the last thing she had expected. He *knew* about that?

'You're not denying it, I notice,' Matthew replied almost wearily. 'I had almost convinced myself it might be more mischief on Kathryn's part.' He threw Josie a look that made her heart turn to stone. 'Seems it wasn't.'

'That's got nothing to do with us,' Josie replied croakily. 'Nothing!' She shook her head, hardly able to believe that she had to contend with Matthew finding out about Harcombe Hall on top of everything else. *Craig!* She cursed him silently, wondering whether she could ever trust him again. 'It's irrelevant!' she asserted strongly, and knew that it was the truth.

'It's been your lifelong dream to live here, though, hasn't it?' he persisted. 'You'd been waiting to purchase for a long time, and then I stepped in and pulled the rug right from under you.' Matthew paused, dark eyes assessing Josie's horrified expression. 'Well, I'm sorry about that,' he murmured. 'Truly sorry. But—'

'Matthew no!' Josie frowned, looking closely at the expression on his face. 'Surely you don't think—?'

'Why didn't you tell me, if it had so little bearing on our relationship?' he asked harshly. 'Hell, Josie! Why did I have to find out from Kathryn, of all people?'

'She's not been a particularly nice person,' Josie murmured. 'Not nice at all.' Tears welled up in her eyes and began to trickle silently down her face. This was too much on top of everything else. She looked at Matthew, saw the anguish in his expression, jerked away as he made a move towards her. 'No!' she whispered. 'Let me tell you all of it.' She sniffed and wiped away the tears from her cheeks, searching in her pocket for a tissue that wasn't there.

'Here.' Matthew dived in the pocket of his denims and pulled out a clean handkerchief.

'Thanks.' Their fingers touched. They looked at one another. Matthew drew in a sharp breath and retracted his hand. Josie almost broke down and sobbed then, but she gathered strength and carried on. 'I went to Overton,' she told him, wiping her eyes, 'for the opening of another branch of the agency. I...I had a headache, and I walked to a chemist shop to get some aspirin. I saw Kathryn inside...' Josie paused and blew her nose, not sure whether she'd be able to carry on. She was aware of Matthew, achingly near, very silent—very still, just watching and waiting. 'I didn't particularly want to see her, but...but anyway I did, and...' Josie struggled with a sob, '...and she said hello, and told me...told me that you and she... were...were...' Josie sniffed, working hard not to break down completely. 'She had just bought a pregnancy testing kit. She led me to believe that...that...she was carrying your child.'

'*What?*' Matthew's expression was a picture of angry disbelief. He released a frustrated breath. 'That woman...' he gritted. There was a tense pause. 'And you believed her—just like that?' he asked. His voice was quiet.

'I...' Josie shook her head. 'Yes,' she whispered. 'I suppose I did.'

'You *suppose?*' Now there was a thread of anger in his questioning. 'Either you did or you didn't!'

'It wasn't as simple as that! You don't understand!' Josie replied sharply. She shook her head. 'All those years away—loving you so much, finding you again. Every moment...' Josie looked at him with misted eyes. 'Hardly daring to believe what was happening between us. I was so frightened...so frightened I'd lose you, like I lost you before. And Kathryn...she wanted you so badly—and you had the children as a tie between you, and you were sharing this wonderful house together...'

Josie shook her head, brushing back the golden strands of her hair with a frantic hand. 'I know I should have come to you, talked about it, told you how I was feeling. But all these years...I've had no one. I've learned to cope on my own, to work things out by myself. I've never loved anyone like I love you, and I was frightened,' Josie repeated desperately. 'Frightened that you didn't love me—*want* me, yes, but that wasn't enough. And when Susan started talking about temptation, and the fact that you and Kathryn were alone in the house together... And when I thought about how it was when I left you that Sunday...'

Josie sniffed miserably. 'I passed Kathryn on my way home. And she looked so determined. And I thought later, when she stood outside the chemist with the pregnancy testing kit in her hands and told me she and you were...' Josie shook her head again, steeling herself to look into Matthew's handsome face. 'I've never felt so devastated in all my life,' she whispered. 'Losing the house was nothing compared to the way I felt when I thought I'd lost you.'

Silence filled the barn—even the puppies in that moment chose to be quiet.

'You should have trusted me.' Matthew's voice was husky with emotion.

'I know.'

'You thought she was carrying *my* baby?'

Josie tried to speak, but no words would come. She thought about her hopes and dreams, about the way it might feel to carry Matthew's child inside her—remembered the pain when she'd imagined Kathryn to be pregnant with his child, and nodded.

'*Oh, Josie!*' Matthew heaved a breath. 'She is pregnant, but I can assure you the baby's not mine.'

'I know.' Josie's voice was small. 'Craig called by this evening. He told me... He told me about him and Kathryn. He's ecstatic—can't wait to be a father.'

'Apparently he's in love with her,' Matthew remarked dryly. 'I wish him the best of luck.'

'Kathryn was with him—she apologised.'

'Did she?' Matthew's narrowed gaze rested on Josie's face. 'Well, that's a start.'

'Craig said that you and Kathryn had a talk,' Josie murmured.

'We did. She told me about the baby—said she was sorry she'd made things so difficult for everyone.'

'You weren't surprised—that she was pregnant?' Josie asked.

'Not really. It's par for the course with Kathryn. Now maybe you understand why Julia and Angus didn't choose her to become the children's guardian.'

'I didn't know she and Craig were...seeing each other,' Josie murmured.

'I found out. But only recently, and then by accident,' Matthew admitted. 'I should have told you.'

'Yes.' Josie frowned. 'Why didn't you?'

Matthew's dark eyes held her face. 'Because I was too wrapped up in you to think about anyone else,' he told her huskily. 'Other people's relationships didn't interest me in the slightest—only you. Only us.' There was a moment of tense silence. 'I've never slept with Kathryn,' he asserted forcibly. 'You are the only woman I care about, the only woman I want.' He moved towards her. 'I love you.' His voice was rich with emotion. 'Very much. Do you believe me?'

Josie smiled through her tears. 'Yes.'

'Can I touch you now?' he asked, his mouth curving just a little.

'Yes,' she repeated breathlessly. 'Oh, yes!'

He moved towards her as if in slow motion, his hands reaching out for her, touching her as if for the first time. He cradled her head in his hands and kissed her—lightly at first, his lips no more than a whisper of a kiss, then with slow purpose, his mouth moving over hers, tasting her, drinking in her sweet softness. Josie closed her eyes, her lips parting as desire flamed through her body. The pressure of his mouth increased with each second that passed, and she responded accordingly, revelling in the thrust of his tongue as it explored the moist interior of her mouth, glad of the pressure of his body as she clung to him.

'You don't know how much I love you,' Matthew whispered. 'Maybe you'll never know.'

'Show me,' Josie replied, looking deep into his eyes.

He lifted her off her feet. She was no more than a feather in his arms. 'Where are we going?' Josie whispered, resting her head against his broad chest, revelling in the strength and warmth of his body, so close to her own.

'To the house.' Matthew kissed her mouth. 'Where else?' he added softly.

He pushed open the door of the bedroom and laid Josie down gently onto the four-poster bed.

'Now, where were we?' he murmured, smiling.

Every moment was magical, every movement, every touch a first step on the road towards proving their love for one another. Matthew's lovemaking was all that Josie had dreamt about—and she had been dreaming a long time. Passionate, sensitive, tempting, erotic...

She cried out breathlessly as his touch lingered, as he sought to prolong the ecstasy of the moment. 'Please! Please!' She hardly recognised the sound of her own voice, but her body—she knew that was hers, was aware with every part of her of the overwhelming need to feel Matthew finally inside her.

His mouth travelled over her skin, warm and sensitive, enticing. 'I love you,' he told her huskily. 'Always... My darling...' He rose above her then, full of masculine power, the man she had always wanted, always loved, and Josie reached up her arms and touched his broad chest, arching towards him as he claimed her, gasping as they moved in wondrous union towards that ultimate goal.

And the glory of it just went on and on and on.

'Why are you crying?' Matthew kissed Josie's trembling mouth as they lay quiet and still afterwards. 'Sweetheart?' He looked down into her face and smiled teasingly. 'Don't tell me—you hated every moment?'

'I love you.' Josie hugged him close. 'So much!'

'I love you too. More than life itself...' He kissed her again with renewed passion, his mouth moving urgently over hers. After a long while he lifted his head and, looking deep into Josie's blue eyes, said, 'Marry me?'

She stilled, half afraid that she hadn't heard correctly. 'What did you say?' she whispered breathlessly.

'I want to be with you always.' Matthew stroked her cheek with a gentle finger, brushed his lips across her damp lashes. 'These past few days have been torture without you. I never want us to be apart like that again. Make my life complete—be my wife.'

'Oh, Matthew!' Josie kissed him then, passionately, as urgently as he had been kissing her a moment before. Desire rose from a spark into a flame, then further, deeper, from a flame into an inferno. They embraced as if they hadn't made love in a month, intent on pleasuring each other once again, kissing and touching—joyous in their love for one another, aroused by each and every movement.

When they were quiet, and Josie was cradled sleepily in Matthew's arms, she heard his voice—deep, masculine, with the thread of humour she loved so much. 'I'll take that as a yes, then, shall I?' he murmured.

It was the best Christmas she had ever had. Barely a moment passed by without Josie wanting to stop and pinch herself; she woke up smiling; she sang all the time. The house, it seemed to Josie, was alive with joy.

The children hadn't been surprised by their announcement on the morning of Christmas Eve—nor at the sight of Josie in the four-poster bed beside Matthew. In fact they'd taken everything in their stride, as children are wont to do, leaving Josie with the impression that they'd already thought it a foregone conclusion that she and Matthew would be together.

Josie smiled at the children now, as they lay exhausted beside their respective puppies on the rug in front of a crackling fire. Christmas Day had been a great success: lots of fun and laughter, mountains of good food, and lungfuls of fresh, crisp air. Perfection in an imperfect world.

'Happy?' Matthew asked.

'Delirious!' Josie replied simply. 'You?'

'What do you think?' He placed the drink he was holding onto a nearby table, reached out two hands and touched her hair, stroking and lifting the golden strands back from her face in a beautifully intimate gesture.

'Mmm, that's nice.' Josie tilted her face and looked back at him. 'Everything's working out, isn't it?' she whispered.

Matthew's mouth curved. 'I knew it would.'

'Liar!' Josie smiled as he lowered his head to kiss her. 'I've been thinking about Sheila,' she murmured. 'She'd approve of us, wouldn't she?'

'Undoubtedly.' Matthew's voice was soft. 'She was always singing your praises. I took very little notice, of course—more fool me,' he added, with a smile. 'If I'd known then what I know now...' He stroked back a strand of hair from Josie's face. 'But at the time, well...'

'You were more interested in real women,' Josie responded lightly. 'Not girls with pigtails and braces!'

'You never had pigtails!'

'I had the braces! Anyway,' Josie continued lightly, 'you know what I mean.'

'It's better now,' Matthew asserted. He kissed her again, deeply, lingeringly. 'Much better.'

Josie snuggled close to his broad frame, laying her head on his chest. 'Kathryn and Craig looked happy together, didn't they?' she murmured. 'They didn't stay long this morning, so I thought maybe we could invite them over properly—to have tea or something over the Christmas break.'

'That would be nice. I'm sure Kathryn would appreciate that.' Matthew wrapped his arms around her body, holding her close. Josie heaved a contented breath. She felt wonderfully secure, supremely happy. 'You've forgiven Craig, then—for his indiscretion?' he asked.

'Yes. The way I feel right now, I could forgive anyone anything!'

'Even me—for buying Harcombe Hall?' Matthew murmured. 'When I think back, to the way you were...it explains a lot.'

'I was crazy not to tell you,' Josie murmured. 'But I had such dreams... This house was simply a focus for them.'

'Dreams?'

'You.' Josie glanced towards Josh and Abbie, asleep now in front of the fire. 'A family.'

'I want to make you pregnant,' Matthew told her huskily. 'I want you to be the mother of my children.'

'Children?' Josie twisted round to face him, a smile of delight on her lips. 'How many did you have in mind?' she whispered.

'Oh, let me see now...' Matthew raised dark brows in teasing consideration. 'Six or seven should just about cover it.'

'*Six or seven?*' Josie's eyes were bright. 'Are you crazy?'

'Yes.' Matthew lowered his mouth to hers once more, his lips warm, sensuous. 'About you.'

'I love you,' Josie whispered, in a voice that was husky with emotion. Tears filled her eyes. 'So much...'

'Good, because it just so happens that I love you too.' Matthew placed the flat of his hand against her face and kissed Josie gently on the mouth. 'More than anything.'

MILLS & BOON®

Makes any time special

Enjoy a romantic novel from Mills & Boon®

Presents™ Enchanted™ Temptation®

Historical Romance™ Medical Romance™

MILLS & BOON®

Next Month's Romance Titles

♡

Each month you can choose from a wide variety of romance novels from Mills & Boon®. Below are the new titles to look out for next month from the Presents™ and Enchanted™ series.

Presents™

TO WOO A WIFE	Carole Mortimer
CONTRACT BABY	Lynne Graham
IN BED WITH THE BOSS	Susan Napier
SURRENDER TO SEDUCTION	Robyn Donald
OUTBACK MISTRESS	Lindsay Armstrong
THE SECRET DAUGHTER	Catherine Spencer
THE MARRIAGE ASSIGNMENT	Alison Kelly
WIFE BY AGREEMENT	Kim Lawrence

Enchanted™

BE MY GIRL!	Lucy Gordon
LONESOME COWBOY	Debbie Macomber
A SUITABLE GROOM	Liz Fielding
NEW YEAR...NEW FAMILY	Grace Green
OUTBACK HUSBAND	Jessica Hart
MAKE-BELIEVE MOTHER	Pamela Bauer & Judy Kaye
OH, BABY!	Lauryn Chandler
FOLLOW THAT GROOM!	Christie Ridgway

On sale from 8th January 1999

H1 9812

Available at most branches of WH Smith, Tesco, Asda, Martins, Borders and all good paperback bookshops

COMING NEXT MONTH

SARAH'S GIFT by Caroline Anderson
Audley Memorial Hospital

Having lost her own family, Sarah loved having Matt Ryan and his little girl, Emily, living with her while they were in England. She didn't know that Matt had an inestimable gift for her...

POTENTIAL DADDY by Lucy Clark

Kathryn wasn't sure she liked the professional Jack—brilliant and arrogant—but his private side was a revelation. He'd make the perfect father, but who would he choose as the mother of his potential children?

LET TOMORROW COME by Rebecca Lang

Gerard came to Jan's help when she most needed it, but she found it so hard to trust, she was sure he'd have a hidden agenda. How could he convince her that he hadn't?

THE PATIENT MAN by Margaret O'Neill

Harry Paradine knew if he was patient enough that the right woman would come along. When she finally did, he found Emily Prince less than trustful—but why?

Available at most branches of WH Smith, Tesco, Asda, Martins, Borders, Easons, Volume One/James Thin and most good paperback bookshops

We are giving away a year's supply of Mills & Boon® books to the five lucky winners of our latest competition. Simply match the six film stars to the films in which they appeared, complete the coupon overleaf and send this entire page to us by 30th June 1999. The first five correct entries will each win a year's subscription to the Mills & Boon series of their choice. What could be easier?

CABARET	__	**GONE WITH THE WIND**	__
ROCKY	__	**SMOKEY & THE BANDIT**	__
PRETTY WOMAN	__	**GHOST**	

C8L

Please turn over for details of how to enter →

HOW TO ENTER

There are six famous faces and a list of six films overleaf. Each of the famous faces starred in one of the films listed and all you have to do is match them up!

As you match each one, write the number of the actor or actress who starred in each film in the space provided. When you have matched them all, fill in the coupon below, pop this page in an envelope and post it today. Don't forget you could win a year's supply of Mills & Boon® books—you don't even need to pay for a stamp!

Mills & Boon Hollywood Heroes Competition
FREEPOST CN81, Croydon, Surrey, CR9 3WZ
EIRE readers: (please affix stamp) PO Box 4546, Dublin 24.

Please tick the series you would like to receive if you
are one of the lucky winners

Presents™ ❏   Enchanted™ ❏   Historical Romance™ ❏

Medical Romance™ ❏   Temptation® ❏

Are you a Reader Service™ subscriber?   Yes ❏   No ❏

Ms/Mrs/Miss/Mr ....Initials ....
(BLOCK CAPITALS PLEASE)

Surname...

Address ....

....

....Postcode............................

(I am over 18 years of age)   C8L

Mills & Boon is a registered trademark of
Harlequin Mills & Boon Ltd.